THE
BURNHEART
Redemption

Also by

CHELSEA CURRAN

Unseen Road to Love

THE
BURNHEART
Redemption

CHELSEA CURRAN

SWEETWATER
BOOKS
An imprint of Cedar Fort, Inc.
Springville, Utah

ISBN 13: 978-1-4621-2185-4

Published by Sweetwater Books, an imprint of Cedar Fort, Inc.
2373 W. 700 S., Springville, UT 84663
Distributed by Cedar Fort, Inc., www.cedarfort.com

LIBRARY OF CONGRESS CATALOGING-IN-PUBLICATION DATA

Names: Curran, Chelsea, author.
Title: Burnheart redemption / Chelsea Curran.
Description: Springville, Utah : Sweetwater Books, an imprint of Cedar Fort,
  Inc., [2017]
Identifiers: LCCN 2017050481 (print) | LCCN 2017053299 (ebook) | ISBN
  9781462128785 (epub, pdf, mobi) | ISBN 9781462121854 (perfect bound : alk.
  paper)
Subjects: | LCGFT: Novels.
Classification: LCC PS3603.U7673 (ebook) | LCC PS3603.U7673 B87 2017 (print)
  | DDC 813/.6--dc23
LC record available at https://lccn.loc.gov/2017050481

Cover design by Katie Payne
Back cover design by Jeff Harvey
Cover design © 2018 Cedar Fort, Inc.
Edited by Hali Bird, Erica Myers, and Nicole Terry
Typeset by Kaitlin Barwick

Printed in the United States of America

10 9 8 7 6 5 4 3 2 1

Printed on acid-free paper

To the real men who inspired Adam, Phillip, and Ian.
Thank you for reminding me never to settle for less than
how a woman should be loved—that literary heroes do exist.

And to my sisters, Aleigha and Courtney, whose talent
and wisdom never cease to amaze me and keep me on
the track. I'd use your nicknames, but you'd never let
me live it down if I did. I love you guys.

ONE

$\mathcal{A}$dam felt on top of the world as he sprinted across the green English countryside toward home at Fairbrooke. Despite working in both the orchards and wheat field from noon till dusk, nothing could squelch his excitement for what was yet to come. Tomorrow would be his sixteenth birthday, and he would earn the rite of passage of traveling with his father to Morocco.

Adam's father earned a respectable living in the trade business and held the status of lord of their countryside estate. Adam helped farm most of their own food and maintained the orchards. Inheriting land meant understanding what it meant to run it from every perspective—and that included the skills of their hired workers.

And with that, Adam grew up appreciating the fulfillment it brought him and was stronger because of it, physically and mentally.

Now coming of age, he was ready to learn more about what had fascinated him since he was a small child. He wanted exposure to other cultures, to know the accomplishments of a successful businessman and not just a humble farmer.

Discarding his boots next to the back door, Adam entered the kitchen to wash for supper. He smiled at the bowl of rising dough on the table. Soon enough, the smell of fresh bread would waft through the house.

When he heard his name being called from outside the window, he turned to see Phillip, his younger brother, trudging in through the door.

"You're finished already?" Adam asked, knowing Phillip was on fence-mending duty today. The boy was only fourteen, but he was tall for his age.

"Yes. And no, I didn't pay off Bernard to finish the job," he answered quickly.

"I didn't say you did."

"You were thinking it." Then Phillip's eyes narrowed. "How are you done already?"

Adam grabbed a pitcher of water and lowered his head over the washbasin. "Papa told me to finish as early as possible. He mentioned this morning that there's something he wants to discuss."

Phillip raised his eyebrows. "Ah, the big Morocco voyage."

"Exactly," Adam said, pouring the shockingly cold water over his hair. He ran his fingers through his wet mahogany locks, attempting to look less like a stray dog. "Why else would he wait to officially invite me unless he wanted it to be more *ceremonial*?"

"I doubt it's anything like being invited to the queen's ball," he chuckled.

Adam rolled his eyes. "You know what I mean."

"But if the queen shows up, you will let me know."

"Shut it."

Phillip only laughed as Adam made his way down the corridor to his room upstairs. There he changed into the clean shirt and trousers the housekeeper always left waiting for him on the bed after a day's work. He also donned his waistcoat and the boots he'd shined himself this morning.

Feeling like a true gentleman, he made his way to his father's study and saw the door was open. Both his mother and father sat around the writing desk, waiting for him.

Their expressions appeared solemn and grave as they talked quietly to each other. For his own sake, Adam hoped it had nothing to with him. But tonight, his gut told him otherwise.

He cleared his throat. Noticing him, his parents seemed to relax, but their smiles didn't quite reach their eyes.

"Son," his father acknowledged. "Finished already?"

Adam didn't miss his forced amusement. It wasn't usually intended unless something was weighing on his mind.

"Yes," Adam replied. "Is everything all right?"

His mother answered. "Come and sit with us."

"Darling," his father said to her, "tomorrow he will be a man. He deserves to stand like one if he chooses."

Adam straightened his posture, somehow feeling both pride and apprehension at once.

"For weeks now," his father continued, "your mother and I have been discussing the proper way to say this. But I hope, after all is said, that your heart will be opened to understanding. And I hope you can forgive us one day."

Adam's heart clenched. What could possibly be so dreadful to require his forgiveness?

He waited for his father to continue, but his mother spoke first. "What I have failed to tell you all these years is that . . . I came from a family that had great expectations for whom I was to marry. When I chose a military man without their consent, he did everything in his power to give me . . . to give *us* a good life and prove that he could provide well. That man passed away before I found out I was with child."

Adam could hear the words, but he had trouble understanding. "What are you talking about?"

"I was far from home. I had nothing to my name," she continued. "My family wouldn't take me in. I had nowhere else to go. This man who has raised you since birth . . . found me in the most destitute and troubled times of my life. He took great pity on me—"

"No," his father said, "I saw a beautiful woman who needed my help. And I wanted to give you both everything I had. In return, I received a wife and son who have brought me more happiness than I could've hoped for."

Adam let out a shaky breath. "You're not my real father?"

"Not by birth, no. But I never saw you less because of it."

"But you waited until now to tell me," he said, feeling multiple raw emotions bubble to the surface.

"We didn't want you to grow up feeling out of place in our family, or that we loved you less than Phillip. But your sixteenth birthday is tomorrow, and we felt now was the right time for you to know," his father said.

"We believe everyone has the right to know where they came from," his mother added.

His father sighed and spoke his next words slowly and carefully. "But such things need to be addressed for reasons of foremost importance. I know you were under the impression that the eldest has the right to my shares and land once the time comes to inherit. But in the law-binding traditions of my father, his father, and many before them, it's said the land must go to the first-born son of Garrow blood. It means—"

"Everything goes to Phillip," Adam finished, feeling anger and betrayal carry his words.

"That's not entirely true."

"But it is," he spat. "You both lied to me. You made me believe that I carried the birthright so I'd feel *accepted*? And taking that all away is supposed to make me feel better?"

His mother stood. "We prepared for this, Adam. Phillip will earn some rights and titles, but we altered as much as we could so that both of you will divide it equally. You won't be denied what you can still earn."

Adam heard, but he didn't interpret the same meaning. "Phillip will inherit Fairbrooke, the business, the lands, and dare I say the girl you spoke of marrying me off to," he said. He pictured his brother and the Rosenlund girl together, sitting atop everything he had been promised. "I assume the merger with them is still in effect, so how will I earn an equal share?"

"That we aren't sure of. But we do know you will inherit the Burnheart estate," his father said proudly, as if the ruin of a failed estate was something to be grateful for.

"That's insulting! The land is barren and the house is in shambles!"

His father's voice rose with frustration. "I would expect you to run it the same as if it were *this* house. I am providing you with your own account and resources to rebuild it and your future. You won't do this alone."

"I deserve more than this! I deserved to know about my real father. Where was he from? Where am *I* from?"

His mother reached over the desk for a sealed envelope and offered it to him. "All the information I have about him and your true heritage is there. I saved it for you."

Adam stared at the envelope for a moment and then chuckled without humor. "I thought you would tell me about Morocco, that I'd go and begin the life that was always planned for me. But that life never was mine." His father sighed, and the look in his eyes made Adam's stomach sink further. "It was Phillip's. It always was, wasn't it?"

"You can always choose a different one," his father said. He was trying to be comforting, but Adam didn't feel it at all. "You can still come with me to Morocco—"

"No," he said, instinctively turning to flee the room as fast as he could.

"Son, stop."

Adam did stop, but something in the pit of his stomach was growing. Something a lot darker and uglier was taking over, and he couldn't find the will to keep it at bay.

"If I'm allowed to stand like a man, then I'm allowed to leave like one." Adam turned to look his father in the eyes. "And don't call me son. You are *not* my father."

With those final words, he left for the only place he'd find solitude. Normally after family rows, he'd run to the stable and find a horse to groom. His hopes had been falsely built and then crushed, and he was supposed to just accept it?

All at once, Adam couldn't breathe. The only father he had ever known and loved wasn't his father to claim anymore. His entire foundation had crumbled to pieces, and all he could do was shamelessly cry until he couldn't anymore.

But as he calmed down, Adam had a thrilling, yet terrifying, thought. He no longer had true ties to this place. No real responsibility or duty as much as Phillip did. He was a man now and had the freedom to choose, just like his father—his *adopted* father—had said.

He looked at the envelope in his hand. It had all the information about his birth father and where his true lineage came from. And there was nothing stopping him from setting out on his own and searching them out.

Night had fallen by the time he gathered himself, and he felt completely sure about what he needed to do.

In the kitchen, he found a sackcloth and stuffed whatever food he could into it before heading back to his room. There he grabbed a satchel and packed all the essentials he could carry.

He'd never traveled like this on his own before. And despite his resolve, leaving behind the only family he ever knew tugged at his heart. The least he could've done was say goodbye, but they'd only try convincing him to stay.

Instead, he left a letter for them on his bed, not explaining where he was going, but telling them his intentions of discovering who he could be without their influence. Along the way, he wanted to see the world on his own terms. And if fate would have it, he'd return someday.

On his way out the door, he passed his brother in the corridor, and Phillip stopped to take notice of all Adam's packed possessions.

"Already packing for Morocco, I see," he chuckled, oblivious to the life-shattering truth.

Adam hesitated for a moment. It wasn't Phillip's fault for everything turning out this way. But knowing what he would inherit, Adam couldn't be around to see it.

"Take care of Mama while I'm gone," he told him, and he walked out the front door for good.

Caleb Garrow put a hand on his wife's shoulder as she softly sobbed into her hands. When he first met Lynnette, he saw a beautiful, kind woman willing to work for a living to ensure the safety of her unborn child. She was everything he wanted and needed in his life, and his love only grew from there. Her loving him back multiplied when Adam was born, and since then it felt like paradise to have a son regardless of where he came from.

Adam's reaction was expected, but seeing it now made living with the regret of not telling him years sooner much more difficult. They waited so he could live his childhood years without feeling like an outsider, without feeling like a guest in a generous man's home. Caleb thought he was doing Adam a service by being the father he didn't have. He loved Adam like his own, no more and no less than Phillip.

But he knew what he was taking away by keeping such a secret. He wanted Adam as his sole heir, but his solicitors who helped Caleb manage the estate knew the truth. They knew of the ironclad will of everything being passed down to the first blood-related son. If he challenged it, his land and business would lose credibility, leaving too much vulnerability for takeover. And without his business, he was left with little he could give to his sons to ensure they had a foundation for their future.

Not to mention the Deveraux family had too much interest in his affairs. Despite having greater fortune, they were in constant search for a chink in his armor, knowing his ship numbers were growing and competition was now posing as a threat to them.

Thankfully, Caleb held no shame in his life to give cause for honest men to lose trust in him. But something like this could be fuel for a potential fire. If Adam could understand what was at stake, perhaps he'd show some maturity and acceptance until his eyes were opened to the bright future he could still have.

Throughout the evening, Caleb passed Adam's door, tempted to knock, but Lynnette encouraged him to let Adam cool off and have his space to ponder.

He reluctantly agreed, but close to supper, he had a tray made for Adam and personally brought it to his room. He knocked with no answer at first, expecting to receive the cold shoulder. But after a full minute of silence, Caleb took the liberty of opening the door himself to find it empty.

It didn't take long for Caleb to notice the empty drawer and folded parchment on his bed. He read the letter twice before rushing to the stables to find Adam's horse missing. He then sprinted back to the house to find his wife.

"Lynnette!" he shouted, out of breath and shaken, eventually finding her in the drawing room.

"He ran," Caleb said. "He left a note saying he's gone to the port, and his horse is gone."

"What?" she whispered, tears immediately pooling in her eyes. "Did he say anything about returning?"

"He didn't say. I must go after him. Wait here with Phillip and I'll be back as soon as I can."

Caleb didn't waste any time. The port was half a day's ride away, and Adam already had a few hours on him. Caleb wasn't worried about Adam going off on his own, but he worried about highwaymen. Man or not, no one would hesitate to take advantage of a boy Adam's age. It made him sick to think about the possibilities. How did he not expect this? If he'd confronted Adam sooner, he could've stopped him.

Dawn was breaking by the time Caleb reached the small inn on the side of the road. He often stayed there on his way to the port. His family frequently accompanied him so they could wave him off at the docks the next morning. He hoped Adam had the idea to stop there. But when he entered the establishment, the innkeeper gave him a confused look and said, "Thought you were gone already."

Caleb frowned. "Excuse me?"

"Saw yer son leave not an hour ago."

"And you let him go?" he exclaimed, knowing it wasn't the innkeeper's fault, but upset nonetheless.

"Said he planned to meet ya at the docks, and he wanted a head start. Is there somethin' wrong, sir?"

He thought quickly and decided to put on a calm front until he reached the port himself and sorted this out. "No. I . . . I sent him ahead, but I hoped to meet him here so we could travel together. I suppose he was a little too eager."

The innkeeper shrugged. "He certainly seemed to be, finally joining ya this season 'n all. He's grown into a fine lad."

Caleb could only nod in agreement.

"Are you sure everything's all right, sir?"

"Yes, thank you. I best be off," he said, and he left the inn as swiftly as he could.

But as he was about to mount his horse, his hands stilled on the reins. As much as his heart was telling him to press on, logic told him Caleb wouldn't find him in time.

He hoped for a miracle as he rode until sunrise. But by the time he reached the port, only a few ships were docked, and one was already on the horizon. No crew members or passersby had any knowledge of where Adam was. Caleb eventually found himself standing in the middle of the working crowd, people pushing past him, his spirits crushed.

"May God be with you, son. Wherever you are . . . God be with you."

wo

Six years later

Adam's heart jolted when the familiar scenery came into sight. Dismounting his horse, the smells of wheat and rich soil filled his senses. The summer had just started, and it brought back memories both wonderful and painful.

After sailing around the Caribbean Islands, working in various professions, living in the filthiest quarters, suffering through ailments he didn't know existed, and finally receiving the answers he'd spent years searching for . . . Adam was home.

Standing behind the boundary line of Fairbrooke, holding onto the reins of his newly purchased horse, he didn't feel like he had the right to cross it. But with a deep breath, he took a step forward and found his way into the orchards for old times' sake.

He walked along the outskirts where he was sure to find himself alone until he saw a figure gracefully drop from a thick branch.

His eyes widened when he noticed that the figure was a woman. She pulled a red apple from the pocket of her apron, shined it on her bodice, and took a large bite.

He couldn't imagine any worker showing such lack of decorum on the job. Unless she didn't belong there and was trespassing.

Curious, Adam shouted, "Excuse me?"

She looked about her surroundings until her eyes met his. He could see her eyes widen, even from a distance, and then she took off running in the opposite direction.

"Wait!" he shouted, chasing after the poor girl. If he'd scared her enough for her to report a strange man lurking in the area, he didn't want to face any bad repercussions before he had the chance to reemerge more elegantly.

The woman was quite agile for running in a dress, though by now it didn't surprise him. What did surprise him, however, was how much energy it took for him to reach her. Thankfully, his high stamina and longer stride worked in his favor. In no time, he was at her heels, and his fingers snatched the back of her sleeve. He only meant to stop her, but he wound up pulling her to him, so she collided with his torso.

She let out an "oof!" and stumbled back a little. Only for a brief second did their eyes meet before she kicked him in the shin. He grunted, but it did little to diminish his balance.

"Calm down," he growled. "I'm not going to hurt you."

"You certainly won't!"

Adam chuckled at her attempt to intimidate him. "Says the one trespassing just a moment ago."

"I was not!"

He was about to comment on the apple until, upon closer inspection of the girl, he recognized her features. And his throat tightened.

She wasn't a tenant, nor a worker, but the eldest daughter of Christopher Rosenlund.

He would have guessed her to be nearly twenty now. She had brilliant light hair, held in a loose braid that nearly reflected white in the sun. He didn't know if it was the heat or just exertion that filled her cheeks with such rosy color, but it brought out the deep blue of her eyes.

Despite her casual appearance, she had matured beautifully over time. He was suddenly self-conscious about his uneven scruff, dirty clothes, and tangled hair that hadn't seen a comb in days.

She took a moment to appraise him from head to toe before she declared, "I was *not* trespassing. Who exactly do you think you are to tell me so?"

She had him there. "You're right. I apologize for my actions. They were undignified, and I'll be out of your way immediately."

Her eyebrows furrowed. "That wasn't an answer to my question."

"And no further explanation will be needed once I'm out of your hair for good," he said, hoping there wouldn't be a reason for them to see each other again. He turned on his heel and went straight off to where he left his horse.

"Hold on," he heard her say behind him. "What is your name?"

"A name you would soon forget. Good day, miss."

"Clearly you're a man acquainted with Mr. Garrow," she said, which stopped him in his tracks. "Otherwise you wouldn't be concerned with trespassers."

Adam hesitated. He recalled spending very little time with the Rosenlunds as a child. He didn't think she would remember his face, but it was more than likely she knew what role he once played in her life if she knew his name or family relations.

It was risky, but knowing her attitude toward him just might give him an idea of where he stood with his family before he confronted them.

"I'm passing through and looking for work," he said, which wasn't a lie. "I was hoping to find a suitable job close by. I'm a good farmer."

"Oh, I see," she said, surprisingly without skepticism. She bit her lip, looking slightly vulnerable for the first time. "Please excuse my coarse tongue. I assure you I wasn't trespassing. I *do* work here . . . so to speak."

Adam smirked. "Didn't seem like it when you took off running."

"Well if a strange boy was chasing after you, what would your first reaction be?"

"Well . . . I'd draw a weapon for starters."

"It's too bad I left my sword at home."

That image, combined with her sarcasm, made him chuckle. And to his amusement, a shy smile hinted on her lovely face.

"Yes," he said.

"Yes, what?"

"Yes, I can imagine it. You at the ready, blade in hand as sharp as your tongue."

Her face became serious. "I apologized for that."

"Oh, I wasn't being facetious. Based on your abilities to leap from a tree wearing a dress and talk down to a *man*, one significantly larger than you . . . it wouldn't surprise me if you had some skill with a blade."

"Does that intimidate you?"

"Not in the slightest." He laughed.

She rolled her eyes. "Naturally."

It seemed obvious that she was a bit oblivious to his identity, but now he was curious for a different reason. Why would a woman of her station be so secretive about her own identity and practically flirt with a complete stranger?

"Miss, I fear this unchaperoned interaction might not be the best option in this circumstance."

Now she was the one to smirk. "Why? Are you dangerous?"

"Not at all," he said seriously. "But I would hate to be happened upon and have it taken the wrong way."

"Like the way you happened upon me?"

"Exactly."

"I'm sure you are right." She shrugged. "Then it's good that I am close with the families on these estates, so perhaps I can help you. Do you have a place to stay?"

"That's still to be determined. I've only *just* arrived."

"I see. First of all, your state of dress needs a bit of help. If it's Mr. Garrow you seek, I know he appreciates cleanliness and decent grooming, especially on a first impression."

Adam had to stifle a laugh. It was very clear she was a land-owner's daughter, with a bold way of speaking and an air of arrogance he remembered once having. Yet she seemed kind, with good intentions. He just didn't have time to be her charity project for the day. And the less involved she was, the better it would be for both of them.

"Good advice. I'll be sure to stop into town."

"Or . . . there is a place you can freshen up close by," she said, her voice sounding less regal and more humbling. "The stableman occasionally stays in the barn overnight. He keeps a grooming kit and a washbasin, if you want to save yourself the long trip."

"That's . . . tempting and a lot to offer to a mere stranger," he said, folding his arms in a challenging way. "But I don't think it's your place to offer another man's grooming tools."

"He's a friend of the family. He wouldn't mind."

There was something in her eyes that made him curious. He did need a shave, and a ride into town would take all day. If he learned anything over the years, it was to trust his gut. And right now, his gut was telling him to take the offer.

"And the stableman wouldn't mind?" he asked.

"No." She chuckled.

"You're absolutely sure?"

"Look . . . I have met countless people like you looking for work and being rejected for the simplest of reasons. Many have been rejected and fallen into destitution because of it. I have resources, so whatever opportunity I come across, I won't ignore it. It's plain to see you have good intentions, but I won't impose on your pride. I really do hope it works out for you."

When she turned to leave, Adam stood for a moment chiding himself for his mannerisms. He was so used to pulling information out of people, he forgot that asking nicely would do just fine around these parts.

"Miss," he called out, jogging to her side. "I haven't been around civilized company in a *long* time. I simply fear for your reputation. Again, being seen helping me could very easily be taken out of context."

Her chuckle was small and almost silent. "It's not as uncommon as most would believe. This isn't London. In fact, my father is as much a farmer as he is a landowner, and I'm not royalty who has been treated like a porcelain teacup meant for display only."

"Oh, your father is head of this estate."

She froze, realizing what she said. "Um . . ." She cleared her throat. "Yes. My father is Lord Christopher Rosenlund."

He chuckled. "Then I *must* ask again. Are you sure it's all right?"

"Very sure."

"In that case . . . I wouldn't mind freshening up before I seek employment, and I'm grateful to use whatever you have on hand. A water trough would even be suitable."

"All right, but on one condition though."

He raised his eyebrow. "There are conditions now?"

"I should say so, for all the grief you put me through. Not to mention it is my father's property."

"Good point," he said, gesturing for her to continue. "Are you sure you won't get bored?"

"So far this is the least bored I've been in months." She smiled again, which he noticed was more becoming on her than a scowl. "Let's fetch your horse."

It took him a second or two, but Adam relaxed his shoulders and followed her into the trees. Perhaps a bond between them would mend at least one old tie he'd severed—one that he was starting to regret the more he got to know her.

A slightly awkward silence fell between them until finally she said, "By now I should probably address you with a name."

"This is true," he agreed. "Of course, propriety says we must be introduced by a third party to know of each other's Christian name."

"And who exactly is around to properly introduce us?"

He looked around for comic effect. "Oh dear . . . I guess you're out of luck."

"You're not going tell me?"

"I will if you guess it right."

"That requires far too much time and thought to be worth it." She chuckled. "*Sir* will suffice enough for me."

"Ugh," he grunted. "I'm too young to be called sir. My name is Adam."

She didn't react, which was a good sign that she hadn't recognized him yet. "Adam . . . ?"

"Just Adam."

She nodded. "A pleasure to meet you, Adam."

"Likewise. Now it seems only fair that you would give me your given name."

"No," she said, laughing. "You gave me just one name and I already gave you a name. I'm afraid you're stuck with Miss Rosenlund for now."

"Very well." He shrugged. "I'll just give you an alternative one until then. Let's see . . . I think I shall call you . . . Blossom."

"Blossom?"

"I would've named you Apple, considering the way we met, but Blossom is more suited to you, don't you think?"

She blushed, which was exactly what he was hoping for.

"I suppose," she said shyly. "Your name is fitting also."

"How so?"

"I believe at the beginning of history, a man named Adam attempted to prevent a woman from partaking of the forbidden fruit," she said, pulling out the apple she'd stashed in the pocket of her apron.

Before she could take a bite, he snatched it from her hand. "And if I remember correctly, he partook just the same," he said. Before she could react, he'd taken a large bite.

He offered it back to her, and she eyed it questioningly. Then she smiled and fed it to his horse, who ate it greedily.

The brute gave him a smug look, and Adam rolled his eyes, making the girl giggle. He was in for an interesting afternoon.

*T*HREE

⎯⎯⬦⎯⎯

*W*hen they reached the Rosenlund's stables, Adam remembered them being a little bigger in his youth, but they were still impressive.

"Come inside," she beckoned, showing him past the stalls to a corner where a washbasin, mirror, and small box with a latch were kept.

She took an empty bucket and returned with it full of clear water, ready to be poured into the basin.

"I'm afraid it's the best I can do," she said.

"It's perfect. Thank you."

"I'll just . . . give you a moment."

She ducked outside and disappeared. He appreciated the chance to clean his teeth, rinse his hair, and trim his unkempt whiskers.

Finishing up, he stepped outside to find himself alone and unsure of what to do next. But at last he saw her coming up the path, and he turned to see her appraise him with approving eyes.

"I brought you some bread and cheese. I thought it would be more substantial than a single bite of apple."

"You mean the apple you painstakingly fought for and then so generously fed to my horse?"

She shrugged. "He looked hungry."

"I assure you, he's well fed."

"So far I'm not hearing a 'thank you for the food.'"

He smirked. "Thank you for the food."

He took a bite of bread and didn't realize how hungry he was until he felt its savory taste on his tongue.

"Follow me," she said. "There's an old pavilion nearby, with a nice place to sit while you eat."

She led him back into the trees and took him to a place where the trees grew wilder until they reached a small clearing. It was hidden near a hillside amidst a grove with wild vines that masked it well.

Under the wooden structure, he sat on the bench as he continued to eat his lunch while she nibbled on her own piece of bread.

"You wouldn't happen to be the lost son of the Garrow family now, would you?"

He nearly choked on his food. "What?"

"I remember my father saying something about the eldest son leaving. His name was also Adam."

"Is that so?" he responded, trying to stay as indifferent as possible. "What do you know of him?"

"I was aware of his existence, but I know very little besides hearing about him leaving. His family didn't speak about it much, which left many to wonder and let rumors spread. Some assume him to be dead; others say he set out to become a pirate. But Mr. Garrow personally told me he was looking for something he lost."

A growing pain started in his chest. "I see. Is that why you're helping me? You believe I'm him?"

"I learned quickly to never assume anything upon first sight. But it's still wise to be cautious."

"You say you are close to the family. How did they react to his disappearance?" he asked.

"They took it hard from what I've heard. Mrs. Garrow was ill for some time, and his brother, Phillip, misses him dearly. I can't be certain about Mr. Garrow, but he sounds hopeful that he will return one day."

"What makes him so sure?"

"He probably isn't. But imagine living your life having every-one tell you your son is likely dead. Would you accept that when there is a small chance he's alive and well?"

Adam was dumbfounded. Judging by her elusive behavior and upbringing, he never would've guessed she'd go so far as to question his lineage while revealing information that some would misconstrue as gossip. But in the way she said it, it sounded like the words were intended to be reassuring.

"So what do you believe?" he asked. "Do you see him as a coward who turned on his family?"

"I'm sure he had his reasons. But then again, I don't know the whole story."

"The story is likely not as thrilling as you would hope it to be."

She raised an eyebrow. "And how would you know of it? Aren't you just a traveler passing through?"

At this point, it was useless keeping up the charade, so Adam continued, "The story begins with Lynnette, who was married before she met Caleb Garrow. She was with child when her hus-band died, leaving her entirely alone. Caleb found her and showed compassion, which eventually turned into love. They married before her child was born and decided to pass him off as his own son. A year or so later, a second son was born, and together they lived as one family.

"Caleb, however, looked over a detail that Fairbrooke could only be passed off to the son whose veins ran with Garrow blood. Adam, although being the first born, could not rightfully inherit the title as he was told throughout his life. He didn't even learn he had a different father until his sixteenth birthday."

"I can see why he would feel betrayed."

"Indeed. His father offered him land and other provisions so he wouldn't be left with nothing. But he didn't care much for any of it compared to the lie he'd been living."

"He had every right to be angry. It does seem a little childish to run away from one's identity, but admirable of him to return. As long as his intentions aren't selfish."

"He only wishes for forgiveness."

"Is it possible for him to make it on his own without it?"

"I suppose so."

"Then he only has more to gain than to lose, I would think."

He took a minute to allow her intuitive words to sink in as they sat together in silence. But he noticed a knowing smile form slightly on the corner of her mouth.

"What?" he asked.

"Nothing," she said innocently.

"You smile as if you know something I don't."

Her smile grew wider. "You *are* Adam Garrow."

"I never said I *was*. I easily could have made the whole thing up just to keep you entertained."

"Yes, I certainly believe that," she said with a hint of sass.

"Well if you won't tell me even your whole name, why should I tell you mine?"

She opened her mouth to retaliate, but they both knew she couldn't argue.

"Fine, then I *will* assume you're Adam Garrow."

"Fine," he shrugged. "Whatever helps you sleep at night."

She sighed with heavy frustration, and he couldn't keep from laughing at how easily he could rattle her. Right then, he chanced a look at her to see her brows furrowed a little as she stared into his eyes. "I get it from my mother," Adam said.

"What?"

"My eyes. Surely you were noticing how brown they are."

Shaking her head at the sudden change of topic, she stood and began walking the path toward the stable.

Adam hurried to join her and said, "May I ask you a personal question? I don't know how to say it without sounding judgmental. But I ask with only the desire to understand you better."

"I'm not easily insulted. Odds are I've answered the same question many times before."

"Most women of your age and standing are spending the season in London."

"A season I already had last year. Being a landowner's daughter doesn't exactly make me a desirable courting option. My father has no sons to pass his orchards and lands to. There's a vast variety of knowledge and experience a man needs to take on such responsibilities if we were to keep this land running."

"Then does your family intend to choose a husband for you?"

"Not if I have anything to say about it."

His eyebrows raised in surprise. "You mean to say you're not already engaged?"

"Of course not," she said, giggling. "If I were, then being alone with you would be wholly inappropriate!"

"And you have never been engaged?" he asked, wondering if she was ever told about the contract their fathers had negotiated all those years ago.

"Absolutely not. I am only twenty and have a few more years to figure out that aspect of my life."

He wondered why Phillip hadn't taken Adam's place in the betrothal. Unless it was Adam who created a scandal large enough to force the Rosenlunds out of the deal. For whatever reason, this knowledge made his stomach lurch.

"You are wiser than I was at your age," he said.

She giggled again. "With those whiskers gone, you're not that much older than I am."

"You're not wrong," he shrugged. "Without my whiskers, many of my employers refused to take me on. But all I had to do was show them my hands, and they accepted me very quickly. Took a long time to prove myself. The work was much harsher than I was accustomed to, but eventually it will age anyone until they can't recognize themselves anymore."

"I believe that can be both good and bad at the same time."

He nodded in agreement. "If I were Adam Garrow . . . you would have spent your time with a man who not only has very little to his name, but willingly abandoned all he held dear for the sake of his pride."

He halted midstride when she suddenly hurried to stop herself in front of him. "We make mistakes," she told him, "but it's how we fix them that determines our identities."

Not just her words but the smile that showed with it was more reassuring than he expected.

"Ah, so you find me charming?"

For a brief moment, he saw mischief in her eyes, but it was soon replaced with curiosity and earnestness.

"I have a gift," she said. "Sometimes I can see a person's intentions very easily. And right now I can see you're a good *man*," she stressed, likely for his benefit, "and no matter what name you have, I harbor no ill will toward it."

"I have good intentions, but I am far from perfect."

"I think you are the first man to admit that."

That made him laugh, and she joined him. The sound of it was uplifting, and he knew how disappointing it would be to never be graced by it again. Like she said, he had less to lose, but much to gain at this point in life.

"Thank you for helping me today, Solana Rosenlund."

"You knew my name this whole time?" she squeaked.

"Absolutely. I just wanted to see if calling you Blossom would make you blush, and it certainly did."

"You, sir, should not tease so boldly."

"You're right, that *was* a bit forward of me. Besides, your given name suits you better. Solana. A ray of sun, which the earth cannot live without."

Her cheeks flushed again and she smiled. They both were quiet as he watched her silently contemplating. The wind blew suddenly, tossing her loose tendrils of flaxen hair about her face, which caused her to look about the swaying tree branches. But his eyes remained on her.

He wasn't usually known for getting lost in a moment, but tentatively, he pushed the hair that fell out of her braid behind her ear. Normally he'd never break such rules of propriety, being alone and hardly knowing each other. But after years away from anything quite so lovely as she—absorbing her kindness and sweet nature—he made a conscious choice and leaned in until he softly pressed his lips against hers.

He half-expected her to pull away and slap him, but in the few seconds he kissed her, he felt her response. And better yet, when he pulled away, he heard her sigh in a way that sounded like she enjoyed it as much as he did.

That kiss, as brief as it was, sparked something that sat dormant for a long time. "I *am* Adam Garrow," he said.

As though she didn't know what to do with herself, she giggled. Yet all too quickly she sobered and stepped away.

"I'm sorry, that was inappropriate of me," Adam said.

She shook her head, her face more crimson now than ever. "No. I . . . I wouldn't have let you if I wasn't curious."

"Was it at least enjoyable?" he asked awkwardly.

"Very much so."

She had a dreamy look in her eyes, and Adam wondered if he had just made a mistake or if he had ruined the best of a moment he might never have again. Either way, he said, "Thank you. For your help, and for listening to my troubles."

"Of course. Will I . . ." She hesitated, but then took a short breath and asked, "Will I see you again?"

In her world, a kiss meant a man wanted to see her again. For scoundrels, it meant something else entirely. But he was no scoundrel, and he had every desire to prove that he wasn't.

"I really hope so. This can't be the last I'll ever see you," he told her.

"Then whatever happens with your family, you'll meet me here again?"

"Absolutely," he said a bit too eagerly. "Tomorrow at noon, I'll be right here at this pavilion."

"Promise?"

"I promise," he affirmed, sincerely hoping he could keep it.

$\mathcal{F}$OUR

————— ⟆ —————

$\mathcal{A}$dam walked his horse past the Rosenlund's boundaries, toward Fairbrooke. He still knew the route that led directly to the front entrance.

All he needed was one moment to say what he needed to say, and if worse came to worst, he knew how to take care of himself from there.

Approaching the front steps, he noticed all the planted hydrangeas in full bloom—his mother's favorite. The familiarity of the sight quickened his steps until he reached the door. He hit the knocker, which gave him a few moments to send a silent prayer before a housekeeper answered.

He didn't recognize her, which somehow made it easier to say, "Good afternoon. My name is Adam. I'm here to call on Mr. Garrow."

"Ah, Caleb or Phillip?"

"Caleb," he said as she motioned him into the parlor.

"Indeed. I believe he is far out on the property, but I will send someone. It's rare that we see surprise visitors not from town, but a pleasure all the same. You may wait while—"

"Adam?" came a voice, and he turned to see Phillip, standing tall, proud and more grown up than he imagined.

Before Adam could get a word out, Phillip strode across the room and pulled him into an embrace that nearly knocked him off balance. Once Adam regained his footing, he returned the hug with equal measure until they let go to really look at each other.

"You're alive," exclaimed Phillip. "And you look well! How is it possible?"

"It's . . . a very long story."

"But here you are. Six years," he said, shaking his head. "We never gave up hope."

"We?" Adam asked.

"We," another voice answered, and he turned again to see the face of the person he likely hurt most of all.

"Mother," he breathed.

Lynnette didn't hesitate either. With tears in her eyes, she rushed forward and pulled her first-born son into her arms. She sobbed into his shoulder while Adam held onto her as if his life depended on it.

"My boy," she said, and he heard her sniff from emotion. "My boy is home."

"I'm home, Mama."

Lynnette pulled back, and Adam noticed a few more lines had been added to her face since he left. Worry lines that he likely caused, including a few streaks of silver in her ebony hair. But she was just as lovely as he remembered.

"But how?" asked Phillip. "What brings you back here after all these years? Are you in some kind of trouble?"

"No, I'm not," Adam assured. "I promise to explain everything, I just . . ."

"You found what you were searching for," his mother answered.

"I did," said Adam. "But I never forgot what I'd left behind. I don't expect to be welcomed back, but I do come to beg for at least forgiveness."

"Nonsense." His mother chuckled, taking his hands in hers. "I already told you. *You're home.* And goodness, you have grown into a fine man."

"With loads of help, I bet," his brother teased.

"Phillip, you haven't a changed a bit. Well, aside from you fitting into your big boy boots. And a baritone voice to match. You actually sound like a man now."

"Amazing what growing up can actually do for a lad."

"I'm sorry I missed it."

He shrugged as though it were nothing, but Phillip's lips pursed whenever he was holding back more than he wanted to express. And Adam couldn't blame him for holding some resentment toward him.

"How is father?" he asked, and he didn't miss the look Phillip and his mother exchanged before they gestured him to follow them onto the grounds. "He's all right, isn't he?"

"He is, physically," Phillip said, "but I won't sugarcoat it . . . he was very upset when he failed to find you at the port."

"Find me at the port? You mean . . . ?"

"He went after you as soon as he found your letter," said Phillip sadly. "He was devastated for a long time. During every voyage, he never stopped looking for signs of you. Sometimes in between his trips, he'd travel to the port and sit at the docks all day."

"If I had known . . ."

"You couldn't have," his mother said. "You did what you needed to do, and at least now we know you're safe."

"Where is he?"

"In the south part of the field today. Near the pond," his mother said. Her expression was reassuring enough for him to make his way through the house. Along the way, he passed familiar furniture and mementos that brought back waves of nostalgia. He went out the back entrance and followed the path that led to the pond not too far from the house.

He passed a few workers pruning trees, and they tipped their caps as he went. Eventually he saw a familiar figure standing on a wooden ladder with his back turned.

Adam approached a short distance behind him and paused a moment. He stood there watching Caleb Garrow picking oranges like he did on his own time whenever he craved them—a sight he'd seen many times as a child, and seeing it again pulled a bit at his heartstrings.

"Mr. Garrow?" he said, feeling a little awkward getting his attention that way, but it felt more appropriate before he had the chance to say his peace.

Caleb stopped what he was doing and descended the ladder without looking back. Finally, he set it down, straightened, and turned. Adam heard his breath catch as he stood motionless for a few heartbeats. After six years, his hair was more peppered with gray than his mother's, his beard was now full and his clothes more casual. But still he appeared every bit the hard land worker Adam remembered him to be.

Caleb's eyes narrowed, as if he were staring at ghost, but had perhaps seen that ghost far too often to give it much attention. But then his eyebrows furrowed, and he began walking toward him with a determined stride, moving faster until he was able to firmly place both hands on Adam's shoulders.

"Adam?" he whispered, both amazement and torture in his eyes.

"Yes," Adam confirmed.

Caleb's face contorted into a scrutinizing expression, jaw almost clenched, as color filled his cheeks. "Was it worth it?" he asked.

Again, that childlike feeling came into play, and Adam almost cowered. Right then he recalled the memory of their last interaction, and he knew exactly what he meant by it. Had it been worth walking out on the man who raised him, to never send word of his whereabouts or if he was even alive and well?

He didn't know if this was the right answer or not, but he could only manage the truth. "Yes. I went searching for my family," he said. "I got swindled into many rough situations along the way. The things I did to survive I'm not proud of, and they are the main reasons for delaying me. But I saw what I needed to see. I saw his headstone."

"Your birth father's headstone." Caleb nodded, his eyes softening a little.

"Whoever he was, I know he left a good impression on the world. I'm proud to be in his lineage. But I had the strongest feeling, as if I'd heard his voice to say to me, 'I sent Caleb Garrow to you for a reason.' And I felt a fool for ever doubting you as my real father. I'm sorry—"

Just like with Phillip and his mother, Adam was abruptly pulled into a tight embrace that was long overdue.

"My son is home."

That was all he needed to say to push the tears Adam had been holding back for years. They spilled over his cheeks now.

"Yes, father."

With one arm kept around Adam's shoulder, he turned his attention to a nearby worker. "Tell the crew they have the rest of the day off and that they can join us tonight for supper. Like the prodigal son, we're celebrating."

"You don't have to," Adam said. "I'm sure there's a lot of things we should discuss."

His father nodded. "Indeed, but I'm hungry. Let's eat first, and we can figure it out later.

Solana sat on her bed to brush her hair, distracted by thoughts of being in the orchard that afternoon. Somehow, she'd ended up in a fantasy that almost didn't seem real. The lost Garrow son roaming about the orchards, as charming as ever and bold enough to steal a kiss. Her first kiss!

She had to think reasonably. A lot could happen overnight, and she wasn't a stranger to the ways of a man weathered by travel and exposure to the world. But that kiss felt special. Whether it was special to him or not remained to be seen. But for now she couldn't stop herself from daydreaming about seeing him again tomorrow.

There were endless possibilities for what would happen when they met again, including ones that could end badly. Those felt closer to the harsher end of reality, but she pushed them out for the time being.

A soft knock sounded at her door.

"Come in," Solana said, and her sister, Faye, cracked it open.

"I saw you smiling at your plate at supper. Is it safe to ask you what you were thinking about?"

She was only twelve, but Faye inherited the same gift Solana had for reading people's thoughts and emotions. With others, she was usually polite enough to keep observations to herself. When it came to Solana's life, however, she was all too eager to ask.

Solana moved over and patted the coverlet for her to sit down. "I met someone."

Faye bounced onto the mattress, wide-eyed. "Was it a boy?"

She chuckled. "Yes. He may just be a new friend, but only time will tell. Would you like to sleep here tonight?"

Faye nodded and tucked herself under the covers while Solana blew out the lamp. She tried to find sleep, but she lay awake thinking of tomorrow's planned meeting with Adam. Though he promised to be there, she understood how reckless it was to spend time alone with someone she hardly knew. But even so, her curiosity was too strong to keep herself away.

Managing a few hours of sleep, she woke up the next morning determined to finish her lessons and managed to be at the old pavilion with an hour to spare.

Feeling silly about her eagerness, she stood to go for a short walk, but a faint, unnatural noise caught her attention behind the thick of the clearing's edge.

What on earth? she thought, straining her ears.

The sound was repetitive . . . like a metallic object scratching against rock. It also scratched at her nerves, sending chills up and down her neck.

Pulling away the bush, she peered through the trees and found the source. It was a man, and her heart leapt at the idea of finding Adam, but she couldn't see his face. He crouched over a pile of twigs, doing what looked like striking flint with a rock and steel.

After a few more attempts, the spark caught on the dry leaves, and he blew on the smoke that rapidly turned into a small fire. He then picked up a large branch from the burning pile and lifted it in the air like a torch. Carefully, he carried it to one tree.

Realizing what he was doing, she leapt through the bushes yelling, "Stop!"

The man whirled around, swinging the branch, missing her by inches.

"What do you think you're doing? Put that out!"

His face was stricken with something akin to panic. His eyes flitted back and forth from her to the empty bottles strewn around a nearby tree.

As soon as she grasped the idea of his intentions, Solana had no time to stop him. He took the torch and hurled it across the clearing. The flames took to the alcohol-soaked wood, the fire consuming it entirely within seconds—starting a chain reaction that couldn't be stopped.

The words, "What have you done?" were about to leave her mouth when a blinding pain exploded through her head, bringing her to her knees.

She opened her eyes, but her vision was blurred. All she could see were brightly colored lights dancing freely about her.

At first she felt nothing, all sound muffled in her ears. A shadow loomed beside her. She knew it was him, the strange man who did this. And she saw too much. He was going to burn down the orchard. She had to warn everybody.

With all her strength, she willed herself to move, but it seemed impossible. The world was spinning too fast.

Finally, the shadow disappeared, but was soon replaced by a thick haze of black. She made the mistake of breathing it in, only to choke it back in burning, painful gasps. The heat continued to rise, and her body had to make a decision. She had to fight through the pain or surrender to a painful death.

Her eyes flew open, and Solana struggled to her feet. Taking her apron, she pressed the cloth to her mouth.

Please, God, help me find a way out of here.

Suddenly the wind shifted, creating a small break in the flames, just large enough for her to get through.

With one last burst of energy, she pushed herself through the gap, moving as fast as her legs could carry her.

Blinking through her tears, trying to cough out the smoke in her lungs without much success, she kept going. The sky was growing darker, the dry grass felt rough against her skin, the smell of burning cedar filled her nostrils with a mind-numbing intensity.

Her vision was fading fast, and finally the darkness was threatening to take her again. She did all she could to fight it, but she was too tired and weak to keep moving. Eventually she couldn't take it anymore. Her body grew heavier by the second until she fell to her knees . . . defeated.

Slowly, her senses began to disappear one by one. First, her sight, and then feeling. Though the taste of smoke lingered on her tongue, all she could comprehend was the sound of cries in the distance.

Then she felt two strong arms carry her away from the nightmare she fell into. She was weightless and at peace. Then all at once, her breath returned.

Her senses followed too quickly, but what stood out the most was pain. She opened her eyes and was not surprised at all to see who rescued her.

"Thank the Lord," Adam said, pulling her tightly against his chest.

She gasped for air again, and he helped her to lean forward, relieving some of the pressure on her lungs.

"Adam!" a voice called.

His brown eyes moved from hers to the distance. Then, gently, he laid her back down, pulling himself up.

"Don't leave me," she said, her voice hoarse and barely a whisper.

He hesitated, returning to his knees. Although her vision was dimmed, she could still make out the relieved look in his eyes.

He pulled her up so she rested against his side. Taking a deep breath, despite the smoke, she could smell the tangy citrus of oranges on his clothes. It was comforting. It smelled like home during the springtime.

"Adam!" someone screamed again, more desperately this time.

"We're here!" he called back.

The sky was getting darker by the minute from the black stacks of smoke in the air. The firelight's glow became more prominent and cast a silhouette on a figure that hurried into view.

"She's alive," Adam said.

The other voiced cursed. "What happened to you?"

She was also waiting for an explanation, but he ignored the question.

"We need to get her out of here, Phillip," he said.

She felt him shift his arms underneath her shoulders and legs.

"Wait," Phillip said.

"We can't wait! Now please help me."

"Your hand, Adam! You're burned."

"I'm fine," he said, but the coughing fit that followed contradicted what he said. "She needs to be attended to first."

"*I* will take her. Get to the stream and cool your skin."

Without answering, Adam struggled to his feet with her still in his arms. She heard him grunt as her weight was transferred into another set of arms.

"Make sure she's safe," he ordered.

Those were the last words Solana heard until her senses dulled into dim voices and rough movements. Eventually, it grew more difficult to separate reality from her dreams. And through all the fog, she attempted to hold onto the vision of the strange man holding the torch. She tried her best to hold onto it, fighting to stay conscious so she could tell someone what she saw. But like the rest of the world, the vision had slipped away, and she finally closed her eyes in blissful sleep.

$\mathcal{F}$IVE

$\mathcal{P}$hillip Garrow was raised to know how to deal with problems that arose in running a homestead. But after leaving the unconscious Solana Rosenlund to their housekeeper, he felt the burden of responsibility grow heavier. He felt sick having to send someone to notify her family. And even sicker when he rushed back to the chaos with a dozen or so men in a haze of fear, fire, and smoke.

In this area, natural brush fires are rarely heard of, even during the dry season. But the workers knew better than to leave lanterns, pipes, or campfires that weren't fully extinguished. Phillip worried over the likelihood of arson.

"Mr. Garrow!" called one of the tenants, and his attention was brought to a man being dragged toward him on a large canvas.

Phillip rushed over to the circle of people to find his father in the center. He was barely conscious and the burns on his body were noticeably severe.

"What happened to him?" he demanded, kneeling at his side. "Has anyone sent for the physician?"

"Yes, sir. A messenger is on his way as we speak."

Alarmed, he looked around for more answers. "Well?" he shouted.

"We found him struggling near the pasture," John answered. "The gate was open. Our guess is he was trying to set the horses free. He may have gotten too close, which could have injured him enough to get caught in the flames."

"We need to get him out of the smoke. Let's move him inside."

With more help, they were able to carry him to the house where they found Lynnette tending to Solana and two other workers in the parlor.

Phillips's mother had no formal experience, but as the daughter of an apothecary, her knowledge extended beyond anyone in the room. As soon as she saw her husband, Lynnette rushed to his side, eyes wide with worry.

"He's still breathing, but barely," said Phillip.

Lynnette nodded as her hands worked frantically to strip clean cloth for his wounds. "Where's your brother?"

"He's fine," he said, rubbing the dust and ash off his irritated eyes.

"Then fetch him. I want him in my sight."

With only a nod, he moved toward the door and jogged back to the stream. But with how the wind blew, a thick brown haze invaded the air, requiring him to cover his mouth with a cloth and squint through his eyelids.

"Adam?" he called out. No reply. He tried calling out again, but a violent cough took away his voice.

He moved to the water and soaked the cloth, which filtered the smoke, making it easier to breathe through. But he doubted his body could tolerate this much longer.

He pushed through the trees, stumbling over debris until movement in the distance caught his eye.

"Adam?" he called out again.

"Phillip?" a quiet voice responded.

Relieved, he pushed as fast as he could through the trees until he caught his brother by the arm. Adam cried out in pain. Phillip had first assumed his shirt was covered in soot, but discovered it was actually charred all the way through to the skin.

Switching sides, Adam threw his good arm over Phillip's shoulder, and they both made their way toward refuge. When at last the air became breathable, they collapsed onto the grass and coughed until their lungs were sore.

"Is she . . . safe?" Adam panted.

"Yes. But father . . ." He choked, unable to finish the sentence.

"What? What . . . happened?"

He shook his head. "See . . . for yourself."

They only remained sitting for a minute before continuing on until they reached the kitchen. They each took turns, rinsing out their mouths and cleansing their eyes. Adam gritted his teeth as he began to remove his singed shirt encrusted to his red, blistered skin. Phillip helped by pouring water to loosen the fabric, but it caused Adam to grunt and gasp in agony.

The damage extended to his back and chest, but his hand took the worst of it with burns covered the majority of his skin. At least the fingers looked salvageable.

"I want to see father," Adam said.

"As soon as I'm certain you're able."

"I'm able."

"I need to dress your wounds."

"It can wait," he growled, wrenching his arm free and going to search for their father on his own.

Phillip didn't argue. Adam was better off receiving care from anyone else besides him at the moment. Phillip's energy and will to stay calm was depleting, hands too shaky to even work a bandage. But he still followed, hoping to see everyone in better condition.

When Phillip walked in on the scene before him, he stopped in the doorway.

His mother was kneeling on the blanketed floor, her motionless husband's head cradled in her lap. A vice gripped around Phillip's heart, and his breath caught in his throat. Though her grief was silent, her face was wet and pain-stricken. He watched Adam fall to his knees and hunch over as if to pray. But whatever pleading words ran through Adam's mind, it was already too late. Their father was gone.

Right now, Phillip wanted nothing more than to kneel at Adam's side and grieve with them. But there were others injured, and others calling for him to help put out the fire. He couldn't leave them to take care of it alone, regardless of how close to falling apart he was.

Forcing back his pain, he quietly excused himself to find any word on the physician. Instead, he found Christopher Rosenlund, Solana's father, and a few of his tenants transferring her into the back of a wagon.

"How is she?" Phillip asked, fighting back his emotion one second at a time.

"Something's wrong," Christopher answered, with fear only a father could have, which tore at Phillip's heart. "Her head. She's injured badly, and she won't stop spouting nonsense. She can't tell me what happened or recognize my face. She doesn't seem to know her own name."

"Why is she in the wagon?"

"We were planning on taking her home."

"The physician is on his way. It would be faster if she waited here until he does. Anything she needs, I will personally get."

"Thank you," he said. "I hear you were the one who found her."

"I had help," he said, not ready to discuss the specifics of his brother just yet.

"We are very grateful to you."

Phillip nodded and walked slowly across the field to glare into the flames that kept burning against the pale gray sky. He opened his mouth to scream as loud as he could into the wind and smoke. He dropped to his knees and clutched at the dried grass, desperate for something to hold onto as he sobbed over his worst fears being realized. His mentor, confidant, and friend was gone. His father was one of the greatest men Phillip ever looked up to.

Once he was calmed down, he continued looking at the horizon until one of his own staff found him. He helped Phillip to his feet and guided him toward a private area where the physician eventually arrived. He assessed Solana first and then Adam, who needed to be sedated because of the amount of physical pain that was increasing as his shock was wearing off.

Phillip's only job was to care for his mother. He didn't know how long he sat with her. Time didn't seem to feel relevant, but night had fallen by the time he was called in to see Adam. He was in his old room, sitting at the desk chair, covered in soaked cloths.

"He wants me to stay in London so he can keep a close watch over me," Adam grumbled.

"I think you should," Phillip agreed.

He shot him an angry look. "Our father just died."

"Yes, and your skin is damaged. I do not need a doctor to tell me that without proper care, it will affect how you work—how you live. Father would have wanted it for you."

"You can't speak for him."

"Of course I can!" Phillip yelled suddenly. "I was here! You were not! I know him better than anyone else does, besides our mother, and it is now my job to make certain you come out of this whole and healed because I won't lose you too. Despite the hell you put me through, *I won't lose you.*"

His brother nodded, looking down with remorseful eyes. Adam said his goodbyes and was escorted into town where he'd convalesce until it was safe to transfer him.

Phillip stayed behind to find his mother holding onto Caleb's favorite kerchief. "It's like that night all over again," she said.

"I know," he answered. "At least now we know Adam's safe. And this time . . . I can make sure of it."

Phillip spent the next two days preparing for his father's funeral. On his way home from the undertaker's, he desperately needed some time alone and kept on riding until he saw the Rosenlund orchards over the hill.

Right away he had the inclination to see how Christopher's daughter fared after her accident. He couldn't offer much besides support, but he could perhaps finance whatever care she needed.

The stableman approached to see to his horse as Phillip dismounted, and the housekeeper let Phillip inside. He waited in the drawing room. It wasn't long before Christopher showed up with his wife, Margaret, in tow.

"Mr. Garrow," Christopher acknowledged. "What a surprise to see you here, especially after what happened to your father."

Phillip's heart sunk a little further. He hated the constant reminders and was still unable to properly grieve. He took a deep breath and answered, "I feel it my duty to see to the wellness of your daughter."

"That's very kind of you," Margaret said, a sad look in her eyes. "The physician said she will most likely heal, but . . ."

"Her temperature is spiking," Christopher finished. "And she consistently falls in and out of consciousness. She can't keep any nourishment down."

Phillip sighed in both sympathy and worry. "Is there anything I can do?"

"Could you perhaps tell us what you saw when you found her?"

Phillip strained his memory. "Nothing besides her in the field. Considering her head injury, I could only suggest that she may have fallen."

Christopher's eyes narrowed. "Are there any theories on how the fire started?"

"Right now, there are a number of possibilities, but I'm inclined to believe this wasn't an accident. With where the flames originated and how it spread, it seems too . . . calculated. It took a lot of manpower to stop it from spreading to the house."

"An act of an enemy, then?"

"I have none that I know of, but . . . it could be."

"What of your brother?" Christopher said blankly.

Phillip blinked a few times. "Um . . . what of him?"

"I heard from the physician he has returned. He said he tended to him briefly."

"Yes," Phillip drawled. "He returned a few days ago."

"Seems a bit coincidental, his return occurring just before this great tragedy."

Phillip was silent for a long time, knowing the insinuation and that he needed to choose his words carefully. "With what happened to your daughter, I can understand why you are quick to cast blame. But you are accusing my brother of arson on very little grounds."

"That may be so," sighed Christopher. "Regardless, it's too coincidental to not hold suspicion. I know that your family is in mourning, so I won't say any more about it for now. But until there is restitution, we would like for you and your family, Adam especially, to stay out of our affairs."

Phillip bit back an angry retort, reminding himself that even though Phillip had every reason to defend himself, Christopher was a worried father who could only find comfort in Phillip's agreement.

"Though I wish to argue . . . I see no reason why we shouldn't simply leave each other in peace. I would, however, ask for something in return: that you keep accusations to yourselves until someone is proven guilty."

Now it was Christopher that was silent, but eventually he stepped forward and extended his hand. Phillip shook it, creating an unspoken deal that left him feeling more defeated than reassured.

"I do hope your daughter gets well soon," Phillip said genuinely. "We will be praying for her."

That earned him a forced smile from Margaret, but Christopher kept his jaw clenched.

Seeing his cue to exit, Phillip gave them each a nod of farewell and left the Rosenlund house, suddenly understanding the reality that he was no longer the man who deferred issues like this to his father. As the realization set in, Phillip at last lowered his head and cried out all of his repressed emotions.

When his tears finally ran dry, Phillip felt the strong prompting to stand tall, breathe deeply, and take on each day as it came. As desperate as he was to have his father here with him, he was ready to take on the role he'd been prepared for. And today would be that day.

$\mathcal{S}$IX

$\mathcal{S}$olana woke to the sound of birds in the window. She looked over to see Arietta, the family housekeeper, sitting in the rocking chair across the room.

Solana tried opening her mouth to speak, but a coarse cough replaced her words, drawing attention to her dry lips and parched tongue.

"Good heavens," said Arietta. She quickly moved to Solana's side and gently touched her forehead.

"W-what happened?" Solana breathed.

"Drink this." A cup was pressed to her lips, and the feeling of cool water was welcoming. Though she was able to move her limbs slightly, every part of her ached. How long had she been like this?

"My dear, what is your name?"

What kind of question is that? "So . . . Solana."

Arietta exhaled in what appeared to be relief. "Your fever has broken. Oh, my dear, I do believe you're going to be all right."

Once again, Solana tried to speak, but Arietta left the room before she even knew the right question to ask.

What kind of fever did she contract? She couldn't recall feeling any symptoms associated with sudden illness. She tried remembering any events that would lead her to such a state, but only recalled being in the orchard.

Within moments, her mother entered the room and rushed to kneel at her bedside.

"Mama," Solana whispered, relieved to have her in the room.

"Hello, darling," she said, touching Solana's face with her soft, healing hands.

"Mama . . . what happened to me?"

"Oh, do not worry about that right now. Let's get you well. All your questions will be answered in due time."

"No," Solana protested. "Please, tell me."

"Well . . . what do you remember?"

She pounded her fist on the coverlet, the abrupt gesture making her head pound. "I don't know!"

"All right, calm down. Let me fetch your father first. Arietta, please stay with her."

"Of course, ma'am."

Margaret Rosenlund left the room and made her way outside to the courtyard. For the last three days, Solana had suffered a fever and muttered nonsense. She could barely keep any broth down, which left everyone worried that if the fever didn't take her, malnourishment would.

She stopped for a moment to bow her head and say out loud, "Lord, I thank thee for saving my daughter. Please show me what I must do now and keep my husband calm. In Christ's name, amen."

Margaret had to circle the house until she found her husband near the stables, splitting wood. It was an unneeded task, but knew it was his way of releasing stress.

"Chris," she acknowledged, but he ignored her at first. "Christopher!" she said more forcefully. Finally, he lowered his arm and turned to face her. "She's awake . . . *and* she's coherent."

Without a verbal reply, Christopher dropped the axe and speedily followed her back into the house, but Margaret stopped him just outside Solana's bedroom door.

"My dear, now is not the time to tell her what we discussed."

"It needs to be done."

She stayed him by placing a hand on his shoulder. "She is *not* well."

They both walked inside to find Solana sitting up, fatigued, but it was more than what they'd seen in the last three days. Christopher immediately went to Solana's bedside and kissed his daughter's forehead. He held her hand, which encouraged a weak smile from her.

"My dear," he started, "you were in an accident."

Solana's eyes narrowed. "An accident?"

"You don't remember anything about it?"

She slowly shook her head, and Christopher relaxed a little. "I wish I knew exactly what happened, but we believe you fell from a tree and hit your head. Can you recall the last memory you have?"

"I . . ." She closed her eyes and took a deep breath. "I recall . . . being in the orchard."

"Did you see anyone?" he asked calmly.

Slowly she shook her head. "No. I mean . . . I remember seeing faces, but none that stand out from the rest. But I do remember . . ." she said slowly, and Margaret held her breath, ". . . dark clouds. It wasn't raining, but something was going on. There was shouting."

"When you were found, a fire had broken out the Fairbrooke orchards. Mr. Garrow's son, Phillip, was the one who found you unconscious."

"Was anyone else hurt?"

"No one from any of our properties. However, Mr. Garrow . . . I'm afraid he didn't make it."

"Oh no," Solana sighed, tears welling up in her eyes. "What of his wife and son?"

"They are well, but they are in mourning for their loss . . . as well as their land. It's been damaged beyond repair."

"Is there anything we can do to help?"

"We expressed our condolences," Margaret answered. "But for now they would like their privacy. It will take time for normalcy to resume their household, and I'm afraid there isn't much we can do besides provide encouragement."

Solana nodded in understanding. "Perhaps we can extend our funds—"

"We shall do the best we can," Christopher interrupted. "For now you should rest and focus on healing."

"Yes, Papa."

He kissed Solana's forehead again and left the room, leaving Margaret to wonder how Solana would react if she found out what had passed between families in the last three days.

At this point in time, with all the Garrows were dealing with, it was too much to associate with that family. It was more important to keep Solana, and Faye, as protected as possible. And as their mother, Margaret would see it through—whatever the cost.

Adam lay face down on the cot that smelled like medicinal herbs and garlic. Phillip sat in a wooden chair that creaked with every movement, and with the way he kept fidgeting, the repetitive sound was beginning to claw at Adam's nerves.

"Would you settle down?" Adam snapped.

"Sorry," Phillip mumbled.

"What has your breeches in a wad?"

He heard Phillip take a heavy breath before he tossed an opened letter on the pillow beside Adam. "Word from father's solicitor. There is enough money to rebuild some of the damages, but it will require a loan to keep the boats afloat, and come next summer, I may have to captain the ships myself to pay them back."

"That's a lot to take in."

"Yes," he sighed.

"I could be a captain."

Phillip huffed a laugh. "Your arm won't be of any good use by then."

"Says you."

"And three specialists."

"I have to do something," Adam insisted. "You may be in charge, but . . . we're family, and I learned a thing or two about managing a ship."

"Bet you have," he said. Adam didn't miss the bitterness in his voice.

"Listen . . . I know about the deal you made with Christopher. Their silence about my return as long you agreed to break all ties with them."

"And I plan to uphold that agreement," Phillip said sternly.

"I know. But I understand it puts a greater deal of stress on you trying to keep up our reputation."

"Good. Then you'll do well to stay out of their lives as well."

"I cannot make that promise because eventually I will heal, and we both will do everything we can to have the Garrow name respected again. And once that happens, I'd like to make peace with them."

Phillip stood still in silent contemplation until he said, "That actually sounded profound and hopeful. But if you really cared about the Garrow name so much, why didn't you come home sooner? Caleb may have not been your real father, but you still had a mother." Phillip's jaw clenched. "You still had a brother who shared your blood!"

"I didn't truly see that until I visited my birth father's grave. And though I don't deserve it, the Garrow name was a given to me . . . and it is still the greatest gift I've ever received. I cannot change what I did. But I can be here for you now, and you need more help than ever."

Phillip slumped back into the wooden chair, hunched over with his head resting in both hands.

"I'm still angry," Phillip said quietly. "But you're right, I need help. In time I'll forgive you . . . but for now stay in London, heal, and we'll sort things out one day at a time."

He could live with that. "Agreed."

Adam thought he understood true guilt after what he did to his family. But thinking about the promise he made to Solana had left his stomach in constant knots.

She'd been in the orchard when the fire started because he'd asked her to meet him there. Though relieved she survived, the memory of dragging her out of the flames haunted him constantly. He didn't just want to do right by Phillip, but for Solana and the whole Rosenlund family.

"Will *you* settle down?" Phillip said, breaking his own thought process to notice Adam's angst.

"I have an idea."

"Go on."

"Burnheart."

"What about it?"

"The land is still mine, correct?"

Phillip nodded. "If I say so."

Adam smirked at him.

"Yes, it is yours, but it's in no better condition than the orchards. It would take nearly your whole inheritance to work on the structural repairs alone."

"If I'm ever going to marry one day, I need a house to bring my bride home to, won't I? And if building it with my own two hands can prove I will be a strong and hardworking provider . . . so be it. It was the last thing father gave me."

"Mother will be beside herself not having you here."

"I won't be far away. I'll visit when I can, and it'll be weeks before I can even implement a plan with this prolonging my time frame," he said, gesturing to his bandaged hand.

Phillip was right. Taking on such a task wouldn't be easy, nor did it guarantee any chance in making peace with the Rosenlunds.

But at least he could make it right with his father. Alive or not, it was the last tangible thing his father ever gave him, and Adam had nothing left to lose but time.

"I guess there's hope then."

Adam sighed. "I certainly hope so."

SEVEN

After a week in London, Phillip returned to Fairbrooke feeling restless after hours spent in a bumpy stagecoach. Stepping out into the warm June air, he stretched his stiff limbs and walked inside to find his mother on the parlor settee.

Though her expression brightened when she saw him, she smiled through tired eyes and a pale complexion. "Welcome home, dear."

"Hello, mother," he said, kissing her cheek. "Are you feeling well?"

"A bit fatigued, but nothing a nap won't cure."

He pulled out a letter from his pocket and held it out to her. "From Adam."

She happily took the envelope and then asked Phillip, "How was London?"

"After speaking with all those investors, I'm now realizing how overwhelming this truly is. Meeting Richard Deveraux, I understand what father meant by 'looming vulture.' He holds a share in the business, and every other word out of his mouth was a jab at my incompetence. He's waiting for me to fail, so he can swoop in and take whatever scraps I leave behind."

"The trade business isn't easy, but I am proud of you. You're stepping into your father's role as best you can, and in time, you'll feel more confidence as you go. I assume a long rest is in order."

"Later. I've been sitting far too long and promised a few children from the village a footrace rematch."

His mother chuckled, laying a hand on his. "You are a good man, Phillip. Never forget that."

He kissed her on her forehead and left to change from his traveling clothes to something a bit more suitable for exercise.

Once he rode into the village, he left his horse at the livery and meandered through the square. Near the well at the center of the roundabout a group of four children was kicking a ball around the dirt.

Phillip jogged up to them, sliding on some loose gravel as he intercepted a kick. Seeing him, the children cheered in acknowledgment but quickly returned to the game at hand as he passed the ball to Ralston, the youngest of the group. His five-year-old reflexes missed the ball entirely, but he laughed as he chased after it.

"Mr. Garrow, you're back!" said Cecelia. Her sister, Sophie, only giggled. Ten-year-old Thomas stepped forward to shake his hand, and Ralston came running back to toss the ball to Phillip.

"Are you here to race us?" Ralston asked.

"I promised I would," he said. "And this empty square could use a bit more excitement, don't you think?"

"Yes!" they shouted in unison.

"All right," said Phillip, drawing a line in the dirt with his boot. "We start here, and the last one to the livery is a rotten egg."

The five of them took their positions, and Thomas was the one to call out, "On your mark, get set, go!"

Phillip's long stride was no match for any of them, but he held back just enough to let Sophie stay ahead of him. When he noticed Ralston falling behind, he took the lad by the torso and easily lifted him onto his back.

"Hey, no fair!" called out Thomas as Phillip sped past them. The duo kept running until they reached the livery, Ralston cheering the whole way there. But just as Phillip neared the entrance, a woman stepped out. The surprise sent him skidding to a stop, but not soon enough. His momentum lurched him forward, knocking the poor girl off her feet with a loud "oof!"

Iris Westmont lay on the grass, feeling sore and miffed as she looked up at the tall figure that wasn't watching where he was going.

"Sincerest apologies, miss," he said, standing and offering a hand to her.

But when she reached up to take it, a small group of children came running up from behind, and the man strangely told her, "Wait—stay down and close your eyes."

"Excuse me?" she asked, moving to stand on her own.

But when the children approached, the man turned to the children and very loudly asked, "What's this I've found, everyone? It seems we have stumbled upon a lost princess, bewitched by an evil enchantress!"

Abruptly, all rambunctious behavior ceased as they stopped to study her lying on the ground. Realizing she was now a part of the game, she quickly decided to play along and closed her eyes at once.

It wasn't exactly dignified behavior, but the situation reminded Iris of playing with her niece and nephew. She tried to keep herself from smiling when she heard gasps emanating from the group.

"What do we do?" asked a small voice.

A young girl responded, "I know this story!"

"Really? Well tell us, Cecelia. What shall we do to save her?" the man asked.

"There's only one thing we can do, Phillip," Cecelia answered, now giving Iris the name of the man who ran her over. "A knight needs to kiss her!"

Two girls giggled in unison, whereas the boys kept silent, likely busy rolling their eyes.

"A kiss you say?" said the tall man. "Well, now who here is honorable enough to volunteer for such a task?"

"Not me," said a young boy's voice, followed by a sound of disgust.

"Well, what a shame that is for you. It is said that if a worthy man kisses a princess, he will be invincible, and no one will ever defeat him in any battle he may come into. But if you find the task unappealing, I shall have to kiss the fair maiden myself."

Iris's body froze when she heard his words, followed by the giggles of the young girls in the background.

Surely he wouldn't! She could never kiss a man in front of innocent children, let alone a stranger!

But before she could say anything, a little voice spoke out, "I'll do it!"

"Why, Ralston, how noble of you to offer."

"Mm-hmm," she heard the boy say, and then she felt his tiny hands grab hold of her chin. Iris conspicuously sighed in relief. A smile spread across her lips at the small boy's willingness, and without hesitation, she let him kiss her on the cheek.

Knowing it was time to play her part in the story, her eyes flew open to see a boy, no older than five years of age, beaming down at her in gratification.

"It worked! She's awake!" he shouted in her ear.

Iris chuckled. "Thank you, brave one. You have saved me from the clutches of the evil sorceress. I am forever in your debt."

"Does this mean I'm in . . . uh, invin-sable?" he asked her.

"On one condition," Iris said, pointing a finger at him. "You must promise to eat your vegetables so you can grow big and strong like . . . like . . ."

"Like Phillip?" Cecelia suggested.

Iris blushed. "Yes."

Ralston slumped his shoulders in disappointment. "You mean I won't get magic powers until I'm bigger?"

"That is right," Phillip finally answered. "The magic begins only when you're older. Until then, you have to stay out of trouble for it to work."

Ralston looked to Iris for confirmation. "Really?"

"I'm afraid so."

"All right," he sighed. "Phillip, are you invincible?"

"Oh no, I've never found the opportunity to kiss a princess before," he answered.

With the delighted look of an epiphany, Ralston exclaimed, "You can kiss *her*!"

The two girls giggled once more. "Don't be silly," one chuckled. "She's already awake. She can't be awakened again."

"Ah, but I never said she had to be enchanted, did I?" Phillip winked at Iris then, and the butterflies in her stomach took flight. "But I think she's had enough excitement for one day, don't you think, Sophie?"

"That's for certain," Iris breathed.

"All right, children," he said suddenly. "Run back to your mothers before you're missed. I need to escort this princess home safely."

Sophie approached her then. Smiling, she leaned down to where Iris was sitting and whispered, "I know you're not really a princess, but thanks for playing with us, Miss . . . ?"

"Iris," she answered.

Now that the game was over, Iris was now very much aware of where she was—awkwardly sitting in the dirt while Phillip stayed crouched beside her, appearing thoroughly amused. She stood, unsure of what to do next.

"I sincerely apologize," he said, still chuckling. "The silly things I do to keep the local children entertained. You, however, were marvelous."

"Well it does help having experience being enchanted on previous occasions," she bantered.

"Ah, so this happens to you often then?"

"Sadly, yes."

His brow furrowed with intrigue. "How many times would you say?"

"Too many to count, but as you can see it always turns out well in my favor."

"And was it a different man who kissed you awake each time? Or the same one?"

"Oh, Ralston was the first."

Phillip's eyes narrowed, unsure where the game had taken its turn. Iris smiled and continued, "Not every spell is broken with a kiss. In fact, I'm still inflicted with one particular curse."

"What kind of curse?"

She leaned in close as if to tell him a secret and said, "The curse reads . . . any time I seek a moment of peace, I'm doomed to have tall strangers run me over on the street."

He lowered his head as both broke into laughter.

"Again, my apologies. I wasn't looking where I was going."

"Clearly," she said. "But I can see it was for a good cause."

"So your name, Iris . . . as in, Iris *Westmont*?"

"Yes, you know who I am?"

"I heard of Cedric Westmont and his two daughters, one of course named Iris. I, however, didn't know these sisters were royalty," he said, smiling playfully.

"I don't know about that, but we are here visiting the Rosenlund family, and we enjoy the change of scenery."

"Considering I made a bad first impression, may I have the chance to redeem myself by inviting you to dine with me this evening?"

She raised her eyebrows in astonishment. "Forgive me, but I couldn't agree to such an invitation when I barely know your name," she said.

He smiled. "Usually when I mention my name, people tend to know more about me than I do myself."

"Then you must be popular. But since I'm not from around here, I'm not entirely familiar with it."

"Touché. That does give you reason to doubt my good nature, especially now that I'm more familiar with you than you most likely wanted." She giggled, and he seemed pleased with her response. "Well," he said, "then allow me to make it easier. My name is Phillip Garrow. I own the estate nearby, and—"

"Wait, you *own* the estate? You're *Lord* Phillip Garrow?"

"Ah, so you *have* heard of me. I guess I'm not what you expected."

"Well . . . no," she said honestly. "I assumed you'd be . . ."

"Older?" he offered. "Yes, I know. The land, and everything with it, was originally owned by my father. He passed away this last summer in an accident, and I've taken over since. It's just me and my mother now."

"My sincerest condolences."

"Thank you. Now that you know the brief of my story, do I get to hear yours, specifically this evening?"

She smiled at his sincerity. Despite how he was an incredible tease, she fancied the idea of being in his presence again, regardless of how pleasantly nervous he made her feel. "I would have to speak to my father first."

"Is that a yes on your part?"

The hope shining in his eyes made it hard to resist. "Yes," she said.

His smiled widened. "Perfect, I'll go with you."

"Oh, there's no need for you to do that. I don't want to inconvenience you."

"It's no inconvenience. I've been putting off visiting the Rosenlunds for quite some time, and what kind of man would I be if I were allowing a young woman to walk back alone? Not to mention I wouldn't want any report returning to your father declaring that I wasn't brave enough to ask for his permission myself."

Iris blushed, unsure of what proper protocol required for this moment. And apparently her apprehension showed on her face when he followed up with, "I'm sorry if my forwardness is making you uncomfortable."

"No, no. It's a good kind of uncomfortable." Now he looked confused. "The kind a woman feels when she is simply intimidated by an intriguing man who insists on walking her home."

"Intriguing how, exactly?" he asked, his smile indicating pure mischief.

She playfully rolled her eyes and turned on her heels. "And that, sir, is all you will get out of me . . . for now."

"I think it would be the least you could do after I saved you from the enchantress's spell."

She chuckled, as he easily caught her stride. "You forget it was Ralston who broke the curse, not you."

"And I will gladly rectify that now if you'd like." She laughed, knowing he was only teasing. But she was beginning to like the idea more and more.

EIGHT

"You? Courting Iris Westmont?" Adam said to Phillip as he helped him load a shipment of lumber into the wagon.

"What's wrong with that? We've had a number of outings together since we met, and already I can see a future with her."

"Isn't her family close to the Rosenlunds?"

"Yes, and?"

Adam shrugged. "Seems like embarking on dangerous territory."

"Says the man who wishes to court Solana Rosenlund herself."

"It's merely a possibility, only after I begin running my land and earn a real income."

"Things I currently have," Phillip scoffed.

"And what does her father have to say about it?"

"For starters, I spoke to Christopher the same night I declared my intentions for Iris. I was sure he would threaten to break our agreement of staying out of each other's business. But I made an interesting discovery: Solana doesn't know about your existence any more than the rest of the town. Her head injury took away any memory of that tragic day."

Adam dropped the wooden plank he carried into the cart, feeling his heart clatter along with it. "Are you certain he's telling the truth?"

"I really do. I suggested that if he keep quiet about our affairs to Richard Westmont—that we're financially stable, which is true—then all can continue without problems."

"What kinds of problems?"

Phillip flung a piece of lumber into the wagon and let his arms hang at his sides a moment before looking at Adam directly. "The word has spread about your return, and some people are starting to point fingers at you about the fire."

Adam's jaw dropped. "What?"

"No proof can be tied directly to you," he said quickly. "But the main reason I kept you in London was to prove to the solicitors that you were being treated for wounds, and that a man intent on starting a fire wouldn't stay to get burned. They can't arrest you . . . yet. But that is the main reason why associating with the Rosenlunds is *not* a good idea right now. Christopher is not convinced that you're innocent."

"And if he knew Solana was in the orchard to meet me that day . . ."

"I would suspect you'd be shot on sight."

"Brilliant." Adam sighed. "And you would like to marry the daughter of one of Christopher's closest friends? Iris Westmont must be very pretty."

Phillip took a moment to rest and lean against the wagon. "She's beautiful, intelligent, strong-willed, respectable . . . and an artist. No one has ever been able to spark the feeling I get when I'm around her. I don't know how I've managed to gain the approval of her family, but so far I'm happy, and I really want this to work."

Adam threw in the last load and removed his gloves. "Well it's about time. I am happy for you, but are there any other suspects for starting the fire worth investigating?"

"Personally, I would pick Richard Deveraux. He's been after father's shares for a long time. I don't know how exactly he could have done it with his alibi, but I can't get rid of the nagging feeling that he's connected somehow."

"It's a serious allegation, but I trust that you know what you're doing," said Adam.

Phillip was satisfied with the response, and they finished loading the wagon to leave for Burnheart. They rode along the countryside in silence before Adam announced, "I need to apologize to Solana."

"Shot on sight, Adam. We already discussed this."

"What if she *does* remember me? Any girl would pretend not to in fear of reprimand from her father. I would have."

"That is a theory you shouldn't try to prove."

"And why not?" he exclaimed. "You're not telling the truth about who really helped her that day. I got these burns for a reason, Phillip! Christopher just might be more accepting—"

Phillip let out an exasperated sigh. "It's far too risky, Adam. You may have helped her, but you cannot prove that you didn't compromise her when you first met. If Solana doesn't remember you, she can't deny it, and our peaceful understanding is over. So I beg you, give it some time, wait until the investigation is over, and let things fall into place naturally."

As much as Adam didn't want to accept defeat, Phillip was right. Gritting his teeth, Adam snapped the reins. The horses jerked forward at a faster pace down the road, causing Phillip to reflexively catch himself on his seat.

When they reached the shambles of Burnheart, the two of them stepped onto the packed soil and gazed at the massive amount of work ahead of them.

But with every task, Adam knew they had to begin somewhere. So with determination, he rolled up his sleeves. "Find a hammer, Phillip. Let's get started."

NINE

$\mathcal{P}$hillip had spent the better part of his week clearing out debris and rebuilding the foundation. But there was only so much he could help with before he had to plan for his next journey overseas. He finished what he could that morning and left early to make one last trip to the Westmont's home.

When his coach arrived late in the afternoon, the stable hand arrived to take his horses. Phillip encountered him enough times to know his name was Ian O'Connor, a twenty-three-year-old Irish drifter who was looking for work where he could, and who had a gift for breaking horses.

"Afternoon, good man," Ian said, tipping his cap. "Nice to see ya again."

"Nice to see you as well."

"Ms. Westmont is tendin' to the garden out back if ya wish to see her directly."

"Thank you," said Phillip. "Still being treated well?"

"As always," he said, chuckling.

"Well, when the season is over, there's a full-time position on my estate if you plan on moving on."

"I don't think ya can afford me."

"I can certainly afford your talent, but I doubt Cedric Westmont would ever let you go, because of it."

Ian huffed a laugh and more seriously responded, "It's a generous offer and one I'll consider. So far workin' here has been very ideal for me."

Phillip smirked, knowing well he fancied Iris's sister, Abigail. But he decided to save his teasing remarks for later. "I bet it is. Take care, Ian."

He tipped his hat again, and Phillip left him to retreat around the property. The house was a cottage that overlooked vast acres of land. Cedric Westmont bred elite horses for a living, so those acres were filled with dozens of horses ready to be broken or sold.

The beautiful scenery was the perfect backdrop to where he found Iris, digging away at the soil in a pair of gardening gloves.

"Isn't it a bit late in the season to be planting flowers?" asked Phillip, and Iris turned, standing to greet him with a tight embrace.

"They're chrysanthemums, and I'm pulling weeds. They're some of the few that bloom in July."

"Funny how nature works that way."

"Funny indeed," she chuckled. "But I could use a break. Walk with me."

Together they sauntered along the grounds toward the pasture. She already knew about Phillip's upcoming trip and that he was here to see her before he left. But he hadn't told her how long he'd be gone yet.

"Do you really have to go?" Iris asked, her head leaning against Phillip's shoulder.

"Yes," he groaned. "But unfortunately, the trip was extended a bit longer than I first anticipated."

"How long are you talking about?"

"Two . . ."

"Two . . . ?" she prodded.

"Months," he sighed.

"Months!"

"At the most."

"Phillip, to a woman that's two *years*!" she exclaimed. "How is that not long?"

"It *is* long, but it's work that needs to be done. If it's any consolation, I wish I didn't have to go. I wish I could stay here with you."

"Really?"

"Two months without you to look upon, to hold in my arms, and hear your voice . . . just the thought is maddening."

"Of course, all the while you're exposed to the world while I'm left in the castle tower like a damsel in distress."

"How fitting." He chuckled. "I don't expect you to wait for me." He saw her frown and quickly added, "But I hope you will."

She smiled then, which eased his nerves a little. Two months was a long time, long enough for her to meet someone else and forget all about him. Considering how fast it took him to fall for her, surely it could happen to another man. And if she couldn't wait, then he'd lose everything he hoped to have with her one day.

"I'll wait for you," she assured.

He stopped then, stepping in front of her to look into her eyes. "Remember, my lady," he started, "if a man kisses a princess, he will be invincible in any battle he is in. But the magic works both ways."

He took her hands in his and said in a low voice into her ear, "If the princess returns that kiss, she will fall desperately in love with him, and they will live happily together for all eternity."

A shy smile complimented her blush. "And where did you hear this?"

"My mother told me. She and my father are proof that the magic exists."

"Then I cannot doubt it does exist."

"Kiss me, my princess," he whispered. "Kiss me so I may away to battle and return to you in one piece."

"If I kiss you, will it mean I shall have to spend eternity with you?"

"Only if you wish it."

"Good," she said, applying a soft kiss to his lips. His arms wrapped around her waist as her arms clasped above his neck.

With his face close to hers, he whispered, "When I return, promise you will marry me?"

She opened her eyes. "What?"

"I know that we've only known each other for a short while—"

"Yes," she said quickly.

"But I know—"

"No, I mean . . . yes! I promise I'll marry you."

He raised his eyebrows. "You will?"

She chuckled. "It's as the story says: if the princess returns the kiss, she falls desperately in love with him. Fortunately, that already happened the day I met you."

"And I, you."

"Say it to me then," she whispered.

"I love you," he said, the words full of meaning and truth that would last from now to eternity.

"I love *you*," she responded with equal fervor. "Promise you will return to me."

"Always."

Once again, Adam trudged through the Fairbrooke house on an overcast morning that left the atmosphere cold and dreary. Phillip had already set sail, and Adam chose to stay with their mother to keep her company.

He'd just sat down to polish his boots when he heard glass shatter down the hallway.

Adam dropped the rag and sprinted into the washroom to find his mother unconscious on the ground. Pieces of glass from what he assumed was the washbasin were scattered around her.

"Mama!" he called out, grabbing onto her shoulders as he attempted to rouse her awake.

He shifted her onto her back, feeling for a pulse and listened for breath, but couldn't be sure if it was his personal stress that kept him from detecting signs of life or if the unthinkable had just happened.

"Mama?" he whimpered, feeling like a small child again. "Not you too. *Please*, God. No. Not my mother too."

He placed both hands above her chest and repeatedly pressed against her heart. He did so for what felt like an eternity, all the while tears blurred his vision.

Abruptly, a small gasp came from her throat, and Adam leaned down to listen for her breathing. It was weak, but her heart was beating, and color slowly began to return to her face.

He gingerly lifted her into his arms, unable to miss how light and frail she felt, and carried her to her bedroom. Leaving instructions for their housekeeper to watch over her, Adam hurried to saddle a horse and rode as fast he could to the village doctor.

But when he arrived, he didn't have to dismount to notice the sign in the door that read: *The doctor is out.*

Adam pounded his fist on the saddle and pulled the reins to turn back. He galloped down the country road, maneuvering to miss colliding with a carriage. The driver pulled his team out of the way to avoid him, but the carriage was still close enough for Adam to see a familiar face in the window.

His heart lurched, and a small burst of hope forced him to pull the reins, causing his horse to rear. But eventually the horse obeyed Adam's command and took off toward the carriage.

"Stop! Please!" he called to the driver. Naturally the driver paid him a dirty look and increased his speed, but Adam kept with the pace. "My mother needs help!"

"Stop the carriage, Edmund!" a female voice ordered, and to his relief, the driver slowed to a complete stop.

The carriage door opened, and peering above the top was Christopher's wife, Margaret, eyes wide and searching. "Help?" she asked.

"I believe it's her heart. She collapsed at home not an hour ago. Her breathing and pulse are weak."

As her eyes fixed upon his, he could see the struggle within hers. She exhaled a resolved breath and stepped out of the carriage. "Edmund, you must ride to the Harris place where the doctor is doing his rounds."

"You can take my horse," said Adam.

Edmund looked to Margaret with hesitation. "I don't feel right leaving you here, ma'am."

"Mr. Garrow will take me in the wagon to Fairbrooke," she said. "I trust him, and therefore you can trust me."

"Yes, ma'am," he said, and Adam dismounted for Edmund to take over.

Adam moved to take Edmund's place, but he stopped briefly to ask her, "Do you really trust me?"

"I have seen that look of fear in your eyes before. I know it is real when I see it. Now hurry!"

Adam leaned against the doorway, arms folded tightly across his chest. He watched Margaret sit at his mother's bedside. She was awake and responsive, but only just.

After another minute or so, Margaret stood and quietly approached him.

"First and foremost," she started, "we must wait until the doctor arrives and tells us for sure, but from what I gather, her heart is very weak. And . . . she agrees that it may not hold out for much longer."

"No," he whispered.

"I do believe you should write to Phillip."

"No," he said, turning away from her as his whole body felt like it would come apart any second.

"Adam—"

"I can't."

"So instead you choose to keep the truth from him?"

"Can you imagine reading a cold piece of parchment in a strange land overseas and then living in wretched insanity for weeks, not knowing if she is dead or alive, knowing there isn't anything you can do about it?"

Her eyes flickered, but he could tell she was trying to remain indifferent. "Your reasoning is understandable. I can testify that you have only good intentions; however . . ." She lowered her voice to a careful and quiet tone. "He has the right to know now, rather than to come home with the wrong expectation. And I know nothing I can say will be comforting at this time, but I do wish that whatever the outcome, God will grant you peace."

Adam was touched by her words, but only just, when he walked into his mother's room, finding her resting comfortably. Margaret remained in the open doorway as he sat in the chair by his mother's side.

"Is she in any pain?" he asked.

"None that I know of. Just fatigue. I encourage you to speak to her."

"Will you stay?"

Margaret nodded but stood discreetly in the corner.

Adam took his mother's hand. "It wasn't supposed to be like this," he started, saying his words slowly and carefully. "When I came home, I was prepared to live a life of solitude in case I was turned away for spite. But instead, I was welcomed back with open arms, and for a moment I had a bright future—one that included me building a home, finding a wife, giving you grandchildren . . ."

"Even when I am beyond the grave, you had better give me grandchildren," she said, her voice sounding stronger than expected. Her lighthearted words encouraged him to chuckle. "I love you, my son. My last wish was to see you here and well. And now," she sighed, "I want to be with Caleb."

"I know, Mama. I just . . ." His voice cracked a little, but he sniffed back his emotion.

"I cannot choose to stay, Adam. But I can accept where I'm going. At least now we get to say goodbye this time."

Her words broke his heart, but he knew they came from gratitude instead of malice.

"I want you to never forget . . . to be kind to your brother," she said with a weak smile. "He loves you and looks up to you. Watch out for him. It may seem like he has more responsibilities . . . but I know you will be a great mentor, guide, and protector in his time of need."

"Yes, Mama."

"And when you are married . . . never forget to hug and kiss your wife. I mean it. Do it every day. It makes all the difference."

"Yes, Mama."

"Most importantly, Adam . . . love your children the way your father loved you."

"Yes, Mama," he said, closing his eyes as tears began to burn beneath his eyelids.

"I already said something similar to Phillip before he left, but I did write it down in case he needs a reminder." She took a deep breath and sighed. "I'm little tired," she breathed. "I think I'll rest a while."

He nodded. "Yes, you should. I'll wake you when the physician arrives."

"Good night, my son. I love you."

"I love you too, Mama."

$\mathcal{T}$EN

She never did wake. A few hours after her eyes closed, she passed peacefully in her sleep.

Margaret extended her kindness enough to stay until the physician took his mother's body to the undertaker.

Though he hated telling such sorrowful news so impersonally, Adam regarded Margaret's words and sent Phillip the letter. He added their mother's last note to him, hoping it would give him closure and encouragement to stay put until he saw the trip to its end.

Though Adam didn't want to mourn alone, he hoped Phillip would understand it was too costly for him to return this soon. And he hated to be the one to convince him of focusing on trivial matters when they just lost their mother.

The day of her burial, Adam decided to attend the service, but he stayed discreet amongst the crowd, feeling no desire to draw attention to himself while he grieved for the second time.

Only the few who lived within close distance attended. They had wished him well, but they were all mostly tenants that knew him by recognition. In the small crowd, he noticed a few others he recognized. Iris Westmont—his future sister-in-law—was one of them. His heart went out to her. She was genuinely kindhearted and loved Lynnette like her own mother.

When the moment came for his mother to be lowered into the ground, the vicar read a few of God's words, along with a few of his own, and at last it was time to release the handful of soil he held in hand.

He raised his closed palm over her grave, and the world became blurry as reality settled in his mind. He and Phillip were orphans now. Despite how much he'd grown, the feeling of loneliness and grief weighed heavily on his heart. The only peace he felt was in his belief that his parents had found each other somehow in the afterlife.

With that one happy thought in mind, Adam opened his palm and let the soil fall between his fingers.

The service didn't last much longer after that. As people proceeded to their wagons and carriages, he looked toward the overcast sky, almost surprised that the rain had yet to pour for this moment.

He stood for a long while until he felt a gentle tap on his shoulder. He turned his head slightly to catch a glimpse of the last person he expected to see.

"Hello," said Solana, and his breath nearly caught.

Adam wasn't immediately sure how to respond. At first he was lost in the memory of the day they met, her laughter and her blush. But those looks on her face were replaced with only sympathy.

"Hello," he whispered back.

"I apologize for intruding upon your solace. It was brought to my attention that you were related to the late Mrs. Garrow. I wanted to offer my personal condolences."

"Thank you," he said, appreciating the calming sound of her voice, but in that same moment, he glanced in the distance to see her mother, Margaret, looking at them. She was about to make her way toward them when another guest stopped her in conversation.

Right then Adam realized he had a rare window of opportunity.

"Has anyone told you my name?" he asked.

"I'm sorry, no," she said casually. "But . . . you *do* look familiar."

Hope rose in Adam's chest. The idea of her remembering him, or even restarting whatever friendship had begun in the orchard that day, was enough to bring him some kind of comfort he hadn't felt in days.

However, when he opened his mouth to say his name, Margaret had nearly forced her way between them.

"Darling, it's time to leave," she said, already placing her hand on Solana's shoulder to steer her away.

"Yes, Mama, will you please give us another moment?"

"We must leave before the weather turns. I'm sure this gentleman understands," she said, paying him a warning look.

"Of course," he said. "Thank you. It means the world for you to have come and paid your respects."

He looked into Solana's eyes once more. Her gaze lingered and softened a little. It nearly undid him.

"Good day, sir," she said as she was nearly dragged off toward the carriage.

Watching her step inside the trap, he felt defeated. He thought perhaps Margaret would have a change of heart after the kindness she showed him. But clearly the deal for the Garrows to stay out of Rosenlund affairs was still in effect. And Adam felt inclined to continue in his efforts to change their minds.

He had much to prove, but in the names of his father and mother, he'd one day prove himself worthy of their respect.

Adam swung his ax against the tree trunk and stood back to watch it fall. The snap reverberated throughout the clearing just before he saw Phillip's housekeeper, Letty, running toward him as fast as she could in her skirts.

"Mr. Garrow!" she called, frantic and out of breath.

Adam's stomach twisted. Not much could get Letty in such a state, so his imagination ran wild with dire possibilities.

He dropped the ax and met her at the edge of the grove. "Letty, what's the matter?"

"A letter," she panted. "About your brother."

Adam took the envelope from her hand and tore the wax seal of Phillip's official business stamp. It had nearly been a month since their mother's funeral, and this letter was the first one he'd received from him. But reading its contents, he figured out quickly it wasn't written by Phillip.

> *To whom it may concern,*
>
> *We deeply regret to inform you that the* Blooming Iris *was accosted by a ship belonging to Captain Nathanial Melgar and his crew off the coast of Morocco. Those who survived recounted the attack, explaining the capture of Mr. Phillip Garrow. No ransom was held, only a threat of execution without cooperation. Though he was last seen alive, his whereabouts are unknown, and due to Melgar's tenacity for evading arrest, authorities are no longer willing to see Phillip's case as a top priority. We will do whatever we can, but at the moment we can only show concern in these troubled circumstances. As for Mr. Garrow's business affairs, they will temporarily be deferred to another executive in the company until a permanent solution can be reached.*
>
> *With sincere concern,*
>
> *Robert Tolley*

Adam sank to the ground in sudden exhaustion, rereading the letter three more times to be certain he absorbed all the information correctly.

"What is it, sir?" Letty asked.

He held out the letter for her to read, and she gasped in response. "Can anything be done?"

"I don't know." Adam closed his eyes, feeling another boulder of guilt rest atop his already heavy load. "Nathanial Melgar was a captain I served under during my travels. It was very brief, but long enough to learn Melgar is a dangerous smuggler. I thought we parted on good terms, but I don't think Phillip's capture is coincidence. He wouldn't leave the crew alive if he weren't challenging me somehow. And Melgar has a hideout off the Moroccan coast."

"Could he still be alive then?"

"Yes," he said. "And I have no choice but to go after him."

Naturally he was scared out of his mind for Phillip's life, but his determination to save his brother was a rush of adrenaline he'd never felt before. He thought he didn't have a purpose, but it was a promise he'd already made on his mother's deathbed. "Watch out for him," she had said, and if it meant sailing across oceans to do so, he would—if it was last thing he'd ever do.

ℰLEVEN

—◦◦◦—

𝓘an O'Connor had just finished loading the last crate when he saw Abigail Westmont, Iris's older sister. Long sun-kissed auburn hair and blue-green eyes sparkled in the sun as she skipped toward him, holding several jars of what looked like jam preserves.

For quite some time, he'd been looking for work anywhere he could, eventually finding himself that summer breaking in Cedric Westmont's horses.

He learned fast that some people were prejudiced against outsiders from his homeland of Ireland. But Mr. Westmont was still a generous and highly respectable employer. He and his family, including Abigail, treated Ian with the most courtesy out of all, despite his origins. Abigail especially. She had always been kind and gracious to him, initiating conversations with genuine interest in him as person, and he'd grown fond of her since the beginning of his employ.

"Wait!" she yelled, her voice like bells ringing from a church steeple. A little out of breath, she came to a halt and forced the jars into his hands. "I need you to deliver these if you don't mind."

"All right. And to whom will I be deliverin' these, miss?"

"This one is for Mr. Jones and his family, the vendor you're delivering these crates to. This one is to Mrs. Cartwright. She was recently widowed, and she lives very close to town, so it shouldn't be a problem finding her. And this one . . . well . . . this one's for you."

This time *his* eyes widened. "For me? And what reason would ya be givin' me such a delightful gift?"

She blushed. "My father appreciates his workers and asked me to make extra as bribes to keep them around longer. I'm not quite sure why. My recipe is not very appealing compared to others."

"I'll be the judge of that," he said, opening the jar and scooping out a large amount with his fingers.

He chuckled at her expression when he licked the sweet confection off his thumb and said, "Mmm . . . strawberry, me favorite."

She laughed like she hadn't seen someone purposely use poor manners just to make her feel better. But it was true. That jam *was* delicious.

"I'll see it done," Ian said.

She nodded, retaining her smile.

"Then tell your father I'm convinced. I'll stay as long as I am welcomed," he said, climbing onto the wagon.

She giggled at his comment. "It was a pleasure to have officially met you. Thank you . . . for your help."

He smiled at her pleasantries and appreciated her thoughtfulness.

"No problem. I'll be seein' ya, Miss Abigail."

After his deliveries were made, he returned to the estate feeling far more accomplished than he had any other day of work upon his arrival. What made his heart leap was the surprise of seeing Abigail again, this time waiting in the stables as she brushed one of the horses. He unhitched the team and led them back to their stalls to be watered and fed. She turned around, and he rebuked himself to keep it together.

"How did the deliveries go?" she asked casually.

"Just fine. Made every delivery."

"No problems along the way?"

"None."

"Wonderful, I . . . uh, suppose that is it, then," she said, rocking on her heels.

Ian chuckled, knowing she had no reason to be in the stables; he brushed down the horse this morning. And it thrilled him to know he was the reason she lingered.

"If I could be certain of anythin', it's your preserves that keep us in business. And the look on Mrs. Cartwright's face at the sheer thought of ya thinkin' of her was worth the trip alone. You are a very kind person, Miss Abigail."

Abigail tucked her hair behind her ear, looking at the ground when she smiled. "Thank you."

Ian had some years of experience with flirting. But flirting with Abigail was something else entirely. If he had to be honest with himself, he wasn't just fond of her. He fell head over heels for her since the moment she came riding through the pasture on his first day of work.

"But ya don't have to send me with jam just talk to me, ya know," he added, and her eyes flickered a little in surprise, as if she'd just been caught.

She giggled nervously, shaking her head. "I—I wasn't looking for an excuse. I was—"

"Because I enjoy your company regardless of the reason." He stepped forward, closing some of the space between them, but still keeping an appropriate distance from her. Her expression sobered a little, eyes shining with anticipation for what he might say next.

"Forgive me for being bold," he said, beginning to feel unsure if saying something was the right thing to do. But he'd never felt more brave or reckless than he did now, and he didn't want to miss his chance.

"Yes?" she prodded.

"I care about ya . . . as something more than just a friend."

He heard her breath catch, and the corners of her lips curved up slightly. "You do?"

"Very much. Would someone like yourself ever feel that way about me?"

"Why wouldn't I?" she answered simply, as if there were nothing about him that would be considered flawed in her eyes.

"I'm an uneducated poor man still tryin' to make it in this world. Most people here don't take to the likes of me. I sweat all day. I finish work covered in dirt, clothes nearly worn through, and smellin' of horses. After all that, I can't see any woman so polished and refined findin' me appealin' in that way."

"If *I* may be so bold . . ." she began, "you're more handsome to me than any man I've come across in my life," she said, blushing a deep red by the confession.

"Really now?" He raised one eyebrow, exaggerating a smoldering look that made her laugh, just like he'd hoped she would do.

Ian didn't realize how close their hands were until he felt the back of her palm brush his fingers. Impulsively, he took her hand in his and raised it to his lips. He placed a soft kiss to the back of her hand, and once more she sobered, anticipation returning to her gaze.

He began to lean in until a loud snap of a branch sounded just outside the door. The two jumped apart immediately just before another stable hand walked in.

Without a word, the stable hand grabbed the saddle he needed, touching the brim of his cap in acknowledgment. Ian awkwardly nodded back, and Abigail smiled with pursed lips that clearly read "guilt."

"I hope you have a good day, Mr. O'Connor," she said a bit too loudly before exiting the stable altogether.

Ian wanted to follow after her but chose not to press his luck. On one hand, he was ecstatic like any man would be declaring his feelings to a woman and having them returned. But on the other, she was still the boss's daughter. Any kind of future beyond now was near impossible. And he knew Abigail was smart enough to understand that as well.

Solemnly, he returned to his chores, hoping he would have a chance to see her again soon. The rest of the day he was suddenly burdened with a dozen demands that kept him busy until dusk. By the time he finished, the moon had risen high into the night sky, and he looked forward to resting in the bunkhouse.

On his way across the silver lit pasture, he thought about home, the sweet taste of strawberry jam, and the perfume of Abigail's hair. But all thoughts turned to panic when he felt two sets of hands seize his collar, violently ripping him down to the ground.

He tried calling out, but a cloth was placed around his mouth and another around his eyes.

Ian struggled with all his strength as he was dragged forward into the unknown, but fear had gotten the best of him.

It hadn't been long since he witnessed his father similarly being torn away from the comfort of their own home in the middle of the night by strange men.

He feared for what might happen to him by the same merciless, heathen scum who took his father's life for no other reason than being unwelcome. He was forced to watch his father beaten to death, and he relived the memory as he was forced back onto his knees.

Two men took hold of his wrists, and the gag was removed, allowing air to once again flow freely through Ian's throat. Still blindfolded, however, he couldn't see who it was that had taken him away. Someone kicked him in the stomach, and he doubled over with a grunt, still unable to free himself.

"Why . . . why are ya . . . doin' this?" he gasped, feeling his wrists now being secured by rope. At first, he thought it was to bind them together, but when his arms were outstretched at his sides, he realized what they were doing.

Ian was yanked forward by the collar, and his shirt was then torn completely away from his torso. Still blindfolded, he heard footsteps approaching him from behind and stop only a few feet away. There was an eerie silence before a low voice spoke.

"Who do you think you are?" the voice asked.

Ian couldn't hold in the cry that escaped his mouth as a whip tore at his flesh, sending a painfully hot lash across his bare shoulders.

"You think you could come here and compromise Abigail's innocence as if you had the right to?"

In quick realization, Ian knew the reason he had assumed for him being dragged out here was wrong. He wasn't being tortured for the sake of his heritage. "I did no such thing . . . I—Ah!" he screamed, the whip striking him on his lower back.

"You were intent on corrupting her. I have a witness."

"What they say they saw was false!"

Another strike.

"You were hired, all instincts neglected, giving you the benefit of the doubt, but they were right. It was your plan all along. Work hard, become the favorite, and then lure her into your trap!"

Strike.

Sweat beaded on his face. His voice broke in a whisper. "I care for her."

Strike.

"Men like you feel nothing. If you died at anyone's hands, she'll always think of you as a martyr."

A breeze picked up, causing the burn and sting of the open, torn flesh of his back to increase. Ian gritted his teeth in an effort to keep his cries of agony deep inside his chest, tears soaking the cloth that lay over his eyes as the voice reached close to his ear.

"So here is what you're going to do," he whispered. "You will pack your things and leave. Tonight. If you don't, we know where to find you."

Silence. Not even the crickets could be heard after the ropes were cut and the faceless men departed.

Nearly defeated, Ian lay face down in the grass, feeling every sting as the wind touched his exposed skin.

Remembering what his brother's back looked like after taking a whip and his mother worrying about infection, he soundlessly stood up, wiped away his emotions, and walked with every ounce of dignity he had left to the pump near the workman's shed. It was the cleanest water around, and he had to wash his wounds before a fever could set in.

Carefully, Ian grabbed the pail and filled it to the brim. He knelt down and bent over, biting his lip to hold back the grunt as the long gashes split open, and slowly poured the water over his head, letting the water run down his back. He repeated this process several more times before trudging to the cabins to cover the evidence with a clean shirt.

A few of the men were still awake, chatting amongst themselves, ignoring Ian entirely. Apparently, they were discussing their plans for when the season ended, and this distracted moment allowed him to dress his wounds before anyone noticed.

"So, Ian . . . are you still planning on waiting out the winter here?" one called out, but Ian was only half-listening. His mind was somewhere else entirely.

"No," he mumbled, thrusting his scattered belongings in a sack. He said nothing more as he dressed in the warmest clothes he had and left for the stable, where his personal horse stayed.

He desperately didn't want to do what he felt was necessary. Never had he given in to the people who threatened him. But to whoever secretly detested his presence, seeing him with Abigail was the final straw. Oddly, his attackers didn't threaten to go to Cedric Westmont. But he supposed it would have denied them the chance to seek for themselves what they thought to be justice.

Ian bit his lip to keep from screaming as he mounted his horse. And he did well to keep himself alert as he rode into the night, making his way to the only place he could think of where he felt welcomed: Fairbrooke.

It was the longest ride of his life. The cool air bit at his face, while every movement caused blinding pain from each wound.

When at last he found his way onto the property of Phillip Garrow, he sighed in relief, near dragging himself to the front entrance.

The housekeeper answered the door in a dressing gown and cap, brows pinched and hands on her hips. "Good heavens, sir. What business do you have at this time of night?"

His teeth chattered. "I need to see Mr. Garrow."

The housekeeper huffed and shut the door, leaving him outside. Desperately, he pounded the door harder, and eventually the door opened again. This time it was a man who closely resembled Phillip standing in the doorway.

"I need to speak with Mr. Garrow."

"I am Mr. Garrow. Unless it is Phillip you're looking for—then I'm afraid you're out of luck."

"What?" Ian asked, suddenly feeling his knees give out.

Adam cursed, helping the collapsed stranger on his doorstep to his feet and pulling him out of the cold. When he shut the door, the man held onto the side table.

"Let's start with your name and what you want with my brother."

"My name is Ian O'Connor. Are you acquainted with the Westmont family?"

"Phillip was to marry Iris Westmont."

"I worked for Cedric as a stableman. I met Phillip often, and many times he offered me a job when I was ready to move on. Well, that day has finally come."

"Were you sacked?" Adam asked, assuming if the man rode all night, he was more likely running away than moving on.

"Some of the men didn't like havin' an Irishman on their turf."

Adam sighed in understanding. "Well as sorry as I am to hear that, I'm sorrier to say Phillip isn't here. After setting sail to Morocco, we received a letter that he's gone missing. You are welcome to stay here and convalesce until tomorrow. But that is all I can offer, I'm afraid."

Ian's expression was pinched in confusion and worry. "Missin'? What do ya mean? Is anyone lookin' for him?"

"So far, just me. I have access to one of Phillip's ships and am heading to the port tomorrow."

"I would like to come with ya," Ian said firmly, attempting to straighten his posture, but he remained slightly hunched.

"Forgive me, but you look in no shape to take on such a journey."

"You know nothing about me, save that I have nowhere else to go and nothin' but time to help."

Adam was torn. It wasn't entirely wise to trust a complete stranger with no references or solid proof that his intentions were genuine. But the way Ian held himself despite the pain he was clearly in, and the fact that he offered his help before asking to be taken care of, was a sign of good faith.

Taking an extreme chance, Adam nodded. "Very well. There's a fire going in the parlor. Warm yourself and get some rest. We set sail tomorrow afternoon."

"Yes, sir," Ian said, proffering his hand.

"It's Adam," he said, reaching out to shake his icy skin. He had a feeling this was going to be an interesting journey. But Adam had to admit he was grateful to not have to go alone.

*T*WELVE

---

*A*bigail donned her nightdress and began combing her hair when a strange feeling started to unsettle her. The hair on her neck prickled as a chill blew in from the window. She looked about the room; every candle was lit. No shadow could conceal a person, and yet she felt like someone was watching her.

She stood to make sure the window was sealed shut when she saw a figure slowly making his way toward the well. The man knelt before the pump and began pouring water, bucket after bucket, over himself. She squinted to see better, wondering why he would do such a thing, until she saw them—the dark, contrasting marks that covered his back.

Her eyes were now adjusted, and she could distinguish who it was as he straightened, his face now visible in the silver moonlight.

Immediately, she fled her room, running down the staircase with no thought as to how improper she looked leaving the house. But as soon as she exited the front entrance, someone grabbed her torso from behind and clamped a hand over her mouth.

"Do not scream," the dark figure growled.

Fearful instinct caused her to struggle, and she even attempted to bite his fingers. Harshly, the stranger let go, but only to shove her against the wall, hand still over her mouth. He wore a wide-brimmed hat, and dark cloth covered the lower half of his face.

Something sharp pressed against her abdomen, and she froze, realizing it to be the edge of a knife.

"I *said* do not scream," he growled, sending a shudder down her spine.

Abigail followed his order, but she couldn't keep her body from shaking in terror.

"He's been watching you," he said, sliding the knife up to her neck, "and he did *not* like what he witnessed earlier today."

Who was he talking about? Did this have something to do with Ian?

"I'm going to let go of your mouth—but make a sound, and this knife goes into that delicate porcelain skin. Understand?" he asked, pressing the sharp edge a little for emphasis.

Abigail nodded slightly, and he released his grip to slide his arm behind her back. "I can see why he'd find you so tempting. But my boys and I cannot allow lowlifes like that Irishman to poison our land. If your dear Irish lover doesn't flee like he should, you will break his heart and tell him to leave this place for good. Understand that?"

Abigail remained motionless, tears spilling down her cheeks as she cried over the understanding. These men were prejudiced against foreigners, and they were likely men she knew closely if they were aware of Ian living on her father's land. She desperately wanted to say no, to challenge him. But they got to Ian already and were serious about their threats. There was little she could do besides comply.

But she must not have answered quickly enough, because he roughly turned her around to face him and forced her up against the wall. She cried out in pain. "Please," she whimpered. "I'll tell him to leave. Just don't hurt him anymore."

"That's a good girl," he said.

Behind him, another man appeared and took her attacker by the arm. For a moment, she thought she was saved, until the man seemed to be an acquaintance of his.

"What did *he* say about leaving her untouched?" he spat. "Now let's get out of here before you screw up again."

Abigail remained shaking on the ground as the newcomer bent close to her ear. "Breathe a word to your father, or to anyone, that we were here, and our boss *will* hunt down the ones you care about. And then he'll find you to finish what this idiot just started."

When all was silent, Abigail brought herself to her feet and hurried inside to slam the door behind her. Sure that it was locked, she fell to her knees and silently wept in both heartache and trauma over what just happened to her. She could hardly make sense of it, but it played repeatedly in her mind, highlighting different horrible truths as it went.

When Abigail had stopped crying, she slowly made her way toward her bedroom and crawled under the covers, pulling her knees close to her chest. She was too afraid to dream; fearing the dark voices of those men shrouded her in a world of torment. She hated the idea of complying with her attacker's wishes, but she felt she had no choice.

Without a wink of sleep, Abigail quietly made her way downstairs at the crack of dawn to find Gilbert returning from milking the cows.

"Gilbert, have you seen Ian around this morning?"

Gilbert shrugged. "He took off last night. Once a drifter, always a drifter, I suppose."

Abigail's stomach sank. "Do you know where he went?"

"Beats me. Though he did mention Mr. Garrow offering a job a few times. Could have headed to Fairbrooke, but the chances aren't likely."

That was a chance Abigail was willing to take. "Gilbert, would you please saddle the team and take me to visit Fairbrooke? If Ian is there, he left something behind that I think he would like back."

Gilbert scrunched his nose in apprehension. "What might that be?"

"It belonged to his family," she lied. "And I want to go soon, but going alone would be inappropriate. If you are worried about your duties, I'll ask my father to excuse you this morning."

"Very well. I'll be right back."

Abigail hated lying, but she was desperate and didn't feel comfortable going alone. Once they were on their way, she nervously twisted her fingers until her skin was chapped. A few times she broke down into tears, feeling responsible for putting Ian in the spotlight and feeling wretched over the threat she encountered the night before.

After what felt like hours, they arrived at Fairbrooke. The grounds seemed a bit barren, and she had a feeling there hadn't been much staff around to care for it in the recent months.

"I'll pull around to the stables," said Gilbert. "That's where he'll likely be."

Doing so, they both noticed two men hauling bags into a wagon, and the butterflies in Abigail's stomach fluttered as she recognized Ian.

"Will you wait here for me?" she asked Gilbert. "I won't be long."

Gilbert nodded, and she exited the carriage, pulling her wrap closer to her body. When he finally noticed her approaching, he stopped what he was doing to stare with disbelieving eyes.

"You left," she said, vastly aware of how unkempt she must look.

Ian looked to the other man loading the wagon. The two of them exchanged a nod of understanding, and Ian dropped the sack he carried, gesturing her to follow him far enough away to be seen but not overheard.

"How did you find me?"

"Gilbert told me."

"I didn't want to leave," Ian said softly. "I had a disagreement last night, and I needed to cool off."

"Are you headed somewhere else?" she asked, gesturing to the loaded wagon.

"Just another odd job," he shrugged. "Perhaps I'll return to your father's employ when it's over, and perhaps . . . we could have another chance."

Abigail was resolved on the idea of him leaving. She'd only come to see if he was all right and say goodbye. But the hope in his eyes when he mentioned returning filled her imagination with frightening scenarios. Those men who hurt him wouldn't hesitate to do something like that again, or worse. If she was the reason for it all, she had to put a stop to it. She wasn't worth getting beaten over.

"Ian, I do not think you should return to work for my father," Abigail whispered.

Ian scowled. "You don't?"

"I know the work is good for you. But I don't want you staying for *other reasons*, if there are any."

His scowl deepened. "What other reasons do ya mean? Is this about yesterday?"

"Ian . . ."

"You know I respect you."

"I believe that, but it was foolish to entertain such things, and I don't want you to risk your standing with my father over a silly infatuation."

His eyes fell to the ground, and it was easy for Abigail to read his disappointment. "A silly infatuation . . ."

"Yes," she lied.

"Do you really believe that's what it was?" he said, stepping closer to her, staring intensely into her eyes.

She nodded, and he reached out to place put both his hands on either side of her face. "Then if I kiss ya right now, you would feel nothin'? Because truly, it doesn't seem like ya, Abby . . . havin' silly infatuations with stable hands. But I won't. Not unless ya look me in the eye and say it one last time how ya *really* feel."

"I already told you . . ." she breathed.

"I need to hear it."

She stared him down, blankly. There were no tears, no sadness, just empty emotion as she said, "I don't care about you."

Ian's hands dropped, and he nodded to himself. "I have often wondered how a girl like you wouldn't have found someone by now. But it makes complete sense. Thank you for at least bein' honest."

With those bitter words of anger, he turned and left her, and Abigail didn't stay to watch him leave. She hurried back to the carriage and got in without word.

"Did he get it back?" Gilbert asked. "Whatever he left, that is?"

"Yes," she said. "He has no reason to stay any longer."

"Good for him, I guess."

As they were about to leave, the other man Abigail first spotted jogged up to the carriage window. She hurried to dry her teary eyes and faced him.

"You're Abigail Westmont?" he asked her, and she nodded. "If your sister hasn't received word already, I have an important letter to her regarding Phillip."

"What about him?"

"Best to read this yourself," he said, offering a folded piece of parchment. "Just know we are doing all we can, but I wouldn't have high hopes just yet."

With a polite nod, he jogged back to the stable. Abigail unfolded the letter. If she thought the day couldn't get any worse, it had.

"Gilbert, get back to the house as fast as you can."

THIRTEEN

*S*olana winced a little as her mother pulled on the laces of her corset. Wretched things. If women were meant to have small waists, then God would have given them collapsible rib cages.

"Ouch," Solana grunted, feeling her skin pinch slightly.

"Sorry," her mother said, pulling one more time until Solana was tied in place.

The things I do, she thought. "Remind me, who is hosting this party?"

"Mrs. Higgly is throwing it on behalf of Richard Deveraux and his son."

She said it like that was supposed to mean something to her. "Right, and why exactly are these men being celebrated?"

"It's more of a welcome dinner. Richard was a colleague to the late Caleb Garrow, God rest his soul. Due to the disappearance of his son, Phillip, God *bless* his soul, Mr. Deveraux generously stepped forward and claimed responsibility over the trade business."

"I see," said Solana, feeling like the only one who didn't understand why a spectacle was being made of the Garrow family. And there was only one reason her parents would suddenly want anything to do with them.

"Does Richard Deveraux have a son who happens to be single?" Solana asked.

"As a matter of fact, he does."

Solana smirked. It wasn't that she didn't want to find a husband—or that she wasn't confident either—but she wasn't hopeful. From experience, it was just the way every situation had always turned out. Men didn't want her dowry if they couldn't sell it. It was a bad investment, which is why she wondered what made Richard Deveraux's son stand out enough to make her mother so eager.

At the party, Solana was able to appreciate the paintings and music. But upon entering the dining room, she discovered this event was not as casual as her mother let on. Nearly three dozen people more lavishly dressed than her took their seats, leaving her singled out and feeling plain.

Thankfully she was seated at a table of people she recognized, which allowed for a steadier flow of conversation. She wasn't much interested in the topic until a man stood up from across the room, holding his glass.

"That's Mr. Deveraux," her mother whispered to her, and Solana studied him with more curiosity.

"I would personally like to thank Mrs. Higgly for putting together such a marvelous dinner," Mr. Deveraux announced proudly. "We feel truly feel welcomed, and we hope Wentworth and Garrow's trading company will continue to thrive in the name of its predecessor. Though the circumstances are grave—and we do not overshadow the tragedy that brought us here—it is our goal to help this community. It is our determination to not let the fruits of their labor be for nothing. Let this new start be a memorial to Caleb Garrow and his wife. May they rest in peace."

He raised his glass, as did the rest of guests. As Solana lifted her goblet, she noticed to his right a man who could only be his son.

Though he wasn't as striking as she'd hoped, he wasn't homely—at least as far as she could tell from a distance. But his long hair was pulled back and styled in a French fashion, donning powder that seemed to cover his face as well. Clearly he'd adopted a few fashion trends, which Solana understood, but she didn't exactly find it preferable on a man.

This morning she had fantasized about walking through the orchard with a man only her imagination had configured. But if she had to choose a type, that man would be tall with dark hair, neatly cut, but not too short. Just long enough for the wind to ruffle it and for her fingers to run through the strands she could only hope to be soft and inviting. Never had she'd been *that* familiar with a man, but it was certainly intriguing.

"My goodness," said an older gentleman from across the table. "What has *you* blushing so, my dear?"

"Stuart," said a woman who must have been his wife. "It's rude to acknowledge a lady in such a way."

"Oh no, it's endearing," said Margaret, "to watch today's youth clearly smitten."

Solana scowled in embarrassment. "Mama."

"Camden Deveraux is quite amiable and eligible."

Solana searched for the nearest exit so she could calculate an escape route. Once she spotted the closest doorway, she hurried to stand, but in doing so, a server who was approaching to refill the glasses had crossed her path.

In seconds, the two collided, knocking the pitcher out of the server's hands and all its liquid contents onto Solana's gown.

"Miss, I am so sorry," said the elderly server. But Solana could only focus on the fact that she was soaked from bodice to the end of her skirt.

All eyes were now on her, and Solana didn't hesitate. "It's fine," she murmured as she fled toward the exit.

Naturally she was followed by both the server and her mother. As soon as she was in an empty corridor, she leaned against the wall and let the tears that burned her eyes spill over her cheeks.

"Oh, darling," her mother said, placing her hands on her cheeks.

"I'm fine," she whimpered.

The server stepped in. "Please allow me to help clean your dress. It is all my fault."

"It was an accident," Solana said. "And it's just a dress. I'm tired, Mama. I really want to go home now."

"Pardon me," came a man's voice, and they all glanced over at the man approaching in all his powdered glory: Camden Deveraux. "I saw what happened, and thought I could offer some assistance."

Of course he did, Solana thought. Just when the night couldn't get any worse.

"That's very kind of you, Mr. Deveraux," her mother said a little too brightly.

Frustrated, Solana chimed in. "You know how to launder a gown?"

"Well, um . . . no. But I do have a handkerchief." He pulled out a small white cloth, and Solana forced a smile. She'd read about the clumsy girl and the valiant gentleman coming to her aid. That was their meet cute: the moment they'd start their romantic journey. But all of Solana's focus was directed at her soggy discomfort and the odd powder creases in Camden's forehead. She wanted to take that handkerchief and rub off every grain of powder from his face.

Solana let out an ungraceful snort from the thought, and her mother's eyes widened. "It is kind, Mr. Deveraux. Thank you," Solana said quickly, accepting the gesture. "But I do think it best that I return home and take care of the situation in private."

"Of course. We are still grateful for your attendance," he said, courteously bowing his head.

He left without another word, and her mother sighed. "Well, that could have gone better." She turned to the server. "Will you please send for our carriage?"

"Right away, ma'am," he said, and he rushed off.

When her mother suddenly gave her a scolding look, Solana's eyebrows pinched together. "What's that look for?"

"You did not do that on purpose, did you?"

Solana relaxed but still rolled her eyes. "Yes, Mother. I willingly humiliated myself just to escape another prospect so I can ensure my future of spinsterhood."

"I will let that tone slide for now, but good heavens, child," she groaned. "Do you know how rare and exceedingly perfect this opportunity was?"

"And you think I blew it."

"Well . . ." She placed her hands on her hips and bit her lip. "Not yet, I don't think. He *did* give you his handkerchief—a perfect excuse to meet again so you can return it."

Always leave it to Mother to reap the benefits of any mishap. "Mama . . . I am soaked to my chemise, I feel sticky, and I want to hide under a rock. Can we talk about this another time?"

Her mother's expression softened as she rubbed Solana's shoulders. "I'm sorry, darling. Let's go home."

Though she knew her mother was disappointed, Solana was grateful to have a mother who was at least aware of her feelings and did her best to comfort them. And once they did arrive home, Solana cleaned up and felt relaxed enough to really consider her options. Camden Deveraux *was* kind, and he had some potential to be a good suitor.

But that pesky fantasy that gave her trouble in the first place began to overpower the idea of Camden altogether. It was strange to have it come to her so clearly. Like a memory almost, but hazy.

At least she didn't have to decide on anything. For all she knew, her first impression had turned Camden away, just like all the others. Only time would tell, but for now she made her way to the kitchen for a much-deserved tart.

$\mathcal{F}$OURTEEN

——◦◦◦——

$\mathcal{I}$t was just before daybreak when Adam slumped across the ship's mast in exhaustion. The tempest that almost threatened to overturn them had finally settled.

Although it seemed like the worst was over, lulls tend to happen before horror can pick up where it left off. Adam wasn't going to take any chances. He and the rest of the deck hands worked to salvage what they could and repair damages while they had the chance. Part of it included the torn sail, and Ian was ready to mend it once he helped bring it down.

"Gentlemen," called Captain Spencer, who approached them in his still-drenched overcoat.

The man was in his late twenties—almost too young to be a captain—but his skills were exceptional, and he had a strong voice for leadership. Adam was apprehensive the first few days, but with this cold, frigid weather, he admired Spencer's quick thinking and intuition.

"We should see land by tomorrow morning," Spencer said, rubbing his dark blonde hair with a dry cloth.

Adam exhaled heavily as he coiled a loose rope. "Assuming the storm hasn't set us back."

"Cheery, this one today," he said to Ian.

Ian sighed. "Can ya blame him?"

The captain already knew Adam's story, and thankfully he didn't pester him about it. "We were only set back a few hours, lad. I only came to say that if worse comes to worst . . ."

"I know," Adam said dimly.

"Also, the island you believe Phillip is being held hostage on . . . Do you really know for certain that he's there?"

"It's Melgar's main hideout," said Adam. "Melgar took me there personally . . . and it's when I first mentioned I had a brother to him. It may be a hunch, but after everything I've lost, I can't live on without trying everything.

"Fair enough," sighed Spencer. "I also ask that when you go, you go alone. I will not risk my men facing Melgar."

"I understand."

"Good. Until then, we will have a hearty meal and a much-deserved rest after tonight's fiasco."

"Aye," Adam and Ian both said, and Spencer left them to their duty.

An hour later, the crew sat scattered around deck, eating their breakfast while they shared the same stories Adam admittedly was tired of hearing. While he zoned out, Ian spoke up. "Oi, Captain?"

"Yes?" he answered.

"Do you, or perhaps anyone here, have any instruments?"

"Not that I know of."

He shrugged. "No matter. I'm sure the lot of ya know how to clap a steady beat."

The captain chuckled. "Do you plan on singing for us?"

"I don't sing much, but where I come from, we do have a few traditions I keep close to me heart. Do as I do."

Ian raised his hands and began clapping a steady rhythm. The captain followed and was soon joined by everyone else while Ian moved into a cleared space. He then straightened his posture and began stepping his feet with a speed and precision that took impressive skill. Adam was familiar with this style of folk dancing—mostly in taverns and small village gatherings in his youth—but he'd only managed to learn a few steps, considering it took more years of practice to master.

Ian O'Connor wasn't one to be moody all the time, but this was the first anyone had seen him smile so widely.

After a few minutes, a few sailors joined his side, attempting to mirror the movements but doing a very poor job at it. It increased the volume of the laughter, but it didn't distract from the beat. For some reason, Adam was motivated to join them.

Ian's eyes widened a little in surprise, but when he demonstrated a combination of steps, Adam did his best to follow and was pleased that he had the knack for it. And soon, it turned into a challenge.

It was rare moments like these that Adam refused to take for granted. Though he felt guilty for experiencing any amount of enjoyment while Phillip suffered, these experiences were what kept his emotions balanced. Too much fear or anger would only tamper with his sanity, which he needed now more than ever . . . before everything changed tomorrow.

The next morning, Ian woke up to the familiar creaking sounds of the ship. He rubbed at the short beard on his chin and dressed before walking onto the deck. In the far distance, green trees on the island Adam had navigated them to were present on the horizon.

Near the main sail, Ian found Adam sharpening his dagger. After a few weeks at sea, he'd grown to respect the man as he did Phillip. The two were very much alike, and both could confidently call him friend.

But watching Adam's intent expression on his knife, Ian recognized the tension in his eyes.

"It's not your job to look after me," said Adam, knowing very well what Ian was thinking.

"No, it is not," he agreed. "But if you're allowed to follow your instincts, then I'm allowed to follow me own. Even if it does mean gettin' you out of trouble when you fall into it."

"You say it like it's inevitable," Adam grumbled.

Ian laughed without humor. "It's the way our lives work, lad. I'm prepared to die. It'll still have meanin' this way. But we both know there's more we have to live for. And I'd like to find out what that is, so here's our new deal. I'll have your back if ya have mine. Phillip is top priority, I know. But whatever happens . . . we both come out of this alive."

Ian extended his hand and waited for a response. Adam turned and gave him a hard look but accepted the gesture, silently agreeing to his terms. It relieved Ian to know there was still a hint of sensibility in Adam's eyes.

A few hours later, Captain Spencer found a suitable spot to drop the anchor, while Adam and Ian were given grain, water pouches, two cutlasses, and twenty-four hours before they were to return to let the crew know they were safe.

In a smaller boat, the crew lowered them into the water, and each took hold of the oars. Ian followed Adam's lead since Adam knew the tides better than he did. But while they had time to sit in silence, a question occurred to him.

"How do you know Phillip's here if Melgar's ship is nowhere in sight?" he asked.

"He prefers to dock on the other side of the island."

"Could he be there?"

"I won't discount the possibility. His hideout is on the west-facing cliffs. He stores food and water there, occasionally leaving a few of his lackeys to watch over his cargo. He's only a smuggler of goods, but he does keep the occasional prisoner when a crew member turns on him."

"What's the purpose of holdin' them prisoner? Why not just kill them?"

"Those are only for second offenses. Melgar actually treats his men well since very few men are lining up to join him. If he kills them off, he's a man short. Instead Melgar locks them away, starving and torturing them until he feels their lesson is learned.

Afterward, he shows mercy and grants them their wealth back if they promise to retake their oaths. In the meantime, he finds a temporary replacement, which was me at one point. I was daft enough to think Melgar would actually let me go that easily."

Ian spat in the water with disgust. "Why hasn't he been arrested?"

"He smuggles for the naval war ships."

"Ah, so his front is privateer."

"For the British and the Colonies. He's smart and he's useful."

Once they landed on shore, they both took a few minutes to adjust to solid ground before taking off into the thick of the green wildlife. Although these were desperate circumstances, Ian couldn't help but marvel at his surroundings. He'd seen green before, but the tropical flowers and exotic birds were otherworldly and vibrant.

After thirty minutes or so, Ian finally asked, "Do you know where we're going?"

"I remember the way . . . I think."

Ian rolled his eyes. "Brilliant."

"We've gotten this far, haven't we?"

"We have twenty-four hours to navigate an uncharted jungle!" he pointed out. "Assumin' he *is* here—"

"And assuming we get past the guards on his watch."

Ian stifled a groan, not liking the sound of that at all. "We still need to find our way back to the boat. How far we've come means nothin' if we die out here."

"Cheery, this one today," Adam said sarcastically, and Ian chose to say nothing.

Instead, he pulled out his loaned cutlass and stopped to carve an *X* into a tree trunk. It might make them conspicuous to whatever enemy might be lurking, but taking the necessary risk brought Ian's nerves below the point of anxiety.

Every ten minutes or so, he'd stop to repeat the process, and Adam said nothing about it. He continued to walk the island as if he constantly knew something that pulled him along without hesitation.

"Adam, what do you plan on doin' if we find him?" Ian asked. "You're not a skilled swordsman. You have nothing to trade with. And don't give me the whole speech of takin' his place. Sorry, mate, but you're not worth that much."

"Quiet."

"No, I won't let this—"

"Quiet," he whispered, slowing his pace to gaze up through the trees.

Adam looked back at him in time for Ian to mouth, "What?"

Right now, either Adam Garrow was paranoid, or he sensed something.

"Now is your chance to turn back," Adam whispered.

"No."

"I'm dead serious," he growled.

"So am I."

"You boys quarrel like children," came a voice from behind the thick of vegetation.

Both Ian and Adam reached for the handles of their pistols but didn't draw when a figure wearing a coat covered in bracken and leaves emerged from the trees. He, too, had a pistol in hand, as did the three other men that surrounded them from behind the trees. "Hello, Adam. I see you got Melgar's message," he said.

The man was tall with a strong build, dark skin, foreign accent, a deep voice that held authority, and a stance that demanded respect.

"Ian," said Adam, "meet Captain Melgar's first mate." Then addressing the man, he said, "Neither of us want any harm."

"Of course not. No sane man would come here unless he wanted something."

"I wish to bargain for Phillip's life."

The henchman chuckled. "Son, someone paid Melgar to abduct him. We planned on killing him until we discovered fancy pants was related to none other than our favorite little errand boy."

"What do you want?" Adam asked, sweat now beading at his brow.

"Your first offense was walking out on us."

Adam stepped forward. "He let me go!"

Ian didn't like the sound of where this was going.

"Now, Melgar still has a soft spot for you," the first mate continued, "but these men and I are in the mood for a bit of sport." Again, Ian didn't like the sound of that. "We don't particularly like to shed blood, but we do love a good hunt. Your weapons, please."

Ian felt his dignity draining from him as he handed over his pistol and cutlass, realizing just what these lowlifes wanted from them. "Ya plan to hunt us like animals?"

"You will, indeed, be hunted. But not by us. Too bad our captain isn't here to witness such beautiful irony."

"Adam, what is he talkin' about?"

"I'm really sorry about this, Ian."

The first mate chuckled. "May the best man win."

FIFTEEN

*I*an watched the men disappear into the trees, leaving Adam and him defenseless without a clue what to expect. The first mate said they were going to be hunted, but by what? Were they going to release something and set it loose for Ian and Adam to defend themselves from?

The two stood back to back, moving in a fast circle to keep their surroundings in full view.

"Remember what I said about Melgar taking prisoners?" said Adam.

"Yes."

"I think this is something else entirely."

"Do ya honestly not know how to say a direct thought?" Ian yelled. "What do you mean 'somethin' else entirely'?"

"I think it would be obvious by now! We're being hunted!"

"By what?"

A twig snapped above them, but nothing could be seen. What kind of game were these men forcing them to play?

And right on cue, Adam's shoulder was struck by a blunt object that sent pain extending deep into his arm. In seconds, Adam stumbled backward, a rock no bigger than his palm ricocheting off the side of his head and sending him straight to the ground.

It was remarkable how much information one could absorb in only a matter of seconds, which was just how much time Ian had to discover what they were up against.

Before him stood the remnants of a man who looked very much like Phillip Garrow. His wild hair was matted with grime and dirt and clinging to his chapped skin. There displayed the evidence of torture—scarring wounds and crusted blood exposed through stained, tattered fabric.

"Phillip," said Adam, hurrying to his feet, but his brother didn't respond. He maintained a hardened glare as he lunged forward with a rusted sword in hand.

Ian had little time to react. His body hunched forward as Phillip's blade swung sideways, the tip just missing his belly. Phillip repeated the move from the opposite direction, and again Ian avoided injury by an inch, but it knocked him off balance.

On his back, Ian rolled to avoid being skewered as Phillip went for the plunge. The edge nicked his forearm with a sharp sting just as Adam regained his balance and moved to grab Phillip from behind. One arm was over his shoulder and around his neck, the other seizing his wrist that held the sword. Adam attempted to bend it backward, forcing his grip to open. But in one swift move, Phillip elbowed him in the stomach and lurched forward to fling him over his shoulder.

Ian acted quickly. Already on the ground, he kicked Phillip in the back of his shin, sending him straight to the ground. His eyes still raged with fury as Ian leapt onto his torso to hold him down. His forehead met Ian's nose, and pain dulled his senses a little. His eyes watered, and moisture ran down his face.

Despite having the wind knocked out of him, Adam crawled over to hold down Phillip's thrashing feet. Somehow Phillip had managed to keep an iron grip on the blade that now caused Ian to bleed onto his shirt. He did his best to hold Phillip's wrist down, but Ian had had enough. Adam wouldn't have the heart to do it, so he did what was necessary and raised his body just enough to pull back his arm and throw a swift punch hard enough to knock the poor man out of his misery.

Instantly, Phillip was unconscious, and Adam and Ian slumped in exhaustion. The fight wasn't long, but it took every ounce of physical and emotional energy to bring down a madman.

Adam nearly pushed Ian out of the way, but his concentration was on himself, raising his head to stop the bleeding in his throbbing face. It didn't feel broken, but it would leave a nasty bruise.

"Whatever Melgar did to brainwash him," Adam panted, "it's going to take a while to get him back to normal. Are you all right, Ian?"

Ian nodded, squeezing his eyes shut to correct his bleary vision. But as soon as his sight cleared, he squinted into the trees and noticed figures standing in the branches.

"As amusing as that was, we had hoped for better," came a distant voice. "Guess we'll have to take matters into our own hands, lads."

That's when Ian felt his first real wave of panic set in. They were surrounded and had no way of being able to survive this. He didn't know if it was possible to ask for a miracle now, but in desperation, he whispered, "God, help us."

As if the heavens had made a direct reply, a pistol went off. One of the henchmen grunted and fell to the ground, followed by another. They weren't dead, only injured, but it sparked a reaction that forced Adam to take action.

Five more henchmen, all dressed in primitive clothing as if they were island natives, fell from the trees and came running toward them at all sides. But to Ian's right, the crewman he had come to know over the last month sprang forward in the same fashion. All had weapons drawn, all were ready to engage in battle, and Adam only had moments to throw Phillip over his shoulder and get out of there before being stuck in the crossfire.

Ian followed his retreat. He could only guess that Spencer's crew had taken a second boat after them. God knew they needed a miracle, and the cavalry had been sent. As Ian and Adam moved as fast as they could while carrying an unconscious man through the jungle, the crew slowly trailed behind, defending against their enemy as they moved.

"Ian, you genius man!" Captain Spencer called out, reaching back to fire a shot. "Only you would leave a trail for us to find."

Ian wanted to respond, but he was too distracted by the chaos. He was baffled Spencer and his men would show up after his declaration to keep them from risk.

Gunshots sounded, metal clanked, cries echoed around them, but they all kept running. Eventually they made it to a clearing, but it took them to the edge of a short cliff.

They stopped and looked back to see Spencer's men catching up, and miraculously the henchmen were nowhere in sight. Adam was not far behind, but his adrenaline was depleting. He fell to his knees. Phillip's unconscious body nearly crushed him until someone pulled him off.

"Everyone accounted for?" Spencer asked.

A deckhand answered, "Aye, sir, as he jogged over. "All six, includin' yerself. But the attackers headed south."

"Where the boats are," Ian sighed, resting his hands on his knees.

"They'll have a trap set up by the time we get there," Adam added.

Spencer smiled. "Correction . . . they're headed to where *your* boat is. We docked toward the east side."

Adam scowled. "How did you get to us so quickly?"

"We weren't far behind. Had the impression you needed backup, and I never second-guess myself. Now we must run."

No one had to speak up to agree, but it was Adam who grunted, holding onto his side as he struggled to stand.

Ian was the first to notice why and cursed. "He's wounded. Ya had to take a blade to the side, ya fool."

Spencer was the first to give orders. "Carter, Haynes! You two carry Sleeping Beauty over there. Ian, you take Adam's left arm," he said, taking off his vest. "I'll stop the bleeding with this."

"I can walk," Adam grunted.

"Not fast enough, ya can't," Ian spat. "Come on then."

Running with a man in pain on Ian's shoulder and a determined captain holding a cloth to his bleeding wound was awkward at best. The minutes were long and exhausting, but eventually they made it to the beach where the rest of the men waited for them. But when they got there, Adam cursed.

"Why are you tying him up?"

At the sound of his voice, Phillip began to thrash and yell incoherently as if he were a man being abducted again.

"I've seen this before," said Spencer. "A man tortured, malnourished, and kept in constant darkness . . . He's hallucinating his abduction all over again."

"Captain! Behind the cliff!" someone shouted, and their attention was drawn to the west.

Sure enough, human figures were emerging into view, giving them minutes to get into the boat and be in the water before they were close enough to attack.

"Go!" several men shouted as Ian practically dumped Adam into the boat. Adam struggled to breathe, but he kept up with everyone on the move, pushing the boat into the tide. Once everyone was aboard, they rowed with everything they had.

They were a quarter of the way to the ship when the henchmen caught up. Everyone ducked when shots were fired, but when they drifted too far out of range, the bullets ceased. Once all was quiet, a few laughed hysterically, having just survived a row with the closest thing to pirates they ever faced.

Not only was this whole excursion a miracle in and of itself but also Ian could see in Adam's eyes that more work was still cut out for them. And right away, despite Ian's plans to move on once

Phillip was found, he knew his job wasn't over. Adam needed more help than ever, and Spencer's resources would only go so far.

Resigned in that thought, Ian touched his nose and cringed. His thoughts wandered as they neared the ship. What he wouldn't give to have a full meal, a bath, and a feather bed right now. What he wouldn't give to even just be in that blasted hammock!

But what surprised him the most was how much he wanted to be back working Cedric Westmont's land. Before things went south, it was the happiest place he knew since he migrated. And it had everything to do with the woman he was still hopelessly in love with.

With his life on the line, it was her face, her smile, and her laugh that wouldn't leave his thoughts since the pistols went off. And he doubted those memories would leave anytime soon.

$\mathscr{S}$IXTEEN

$\mathscr{A}$bigail walked into the parlor to find her mother admiring a hair piece made of yellow silk roses.

"Abby!" she said brightly. "Look what just came for you. Are they not lovely?"

Abigail half-smiled, though she was confused as to who would formally send her flowers like these. "Who are they from?"

Her mother held up the card, mischief dancing in her eyes. "Your secret admirer."

Abigail glared at the hair piece. "A bit forward."

Her mother chuckled. "It may not be from a gentleman, but are you not at least flattered?"

"Who delivered them?"

"Bromley went into town to pick up your father's order, and someone had left those for Mr. Wells to pass along."

Abigail shivered. Bromley was Ian's replacement.

Bromley was young, perhaps in his early twenties, and not exceptionally fit to take care of horses. However, he could carry out the basic needs for maintaining the stalls, which was all her father needed for now.

It seemed like lately he was always finding reasons to run into her on the grounds. And when he did, he found some way to ask her personal questions that cause to her wonder what kind of agenda he had.

"They could be from Bromley," Abigail suggested, "pretending they were from an admirer."

"A boy like that wouldn't have the means to purchase silk."

She couldn't argue with that, but there was another option altogether. She still couldn't bring herself to tell her parents what happened to her the night Ian left.

Every day she told herself it could've been worse. Her virtue hadn't been compromised, and she wasn't severely injured. But those men still walked the streets freely, knowing where she lived and how she spent her time. The possibility of being assaulted like that again still hung over her head.

"He's been watching you," he'd said. Which meant he still could be watching her this very moment. It made her feel weak, violated, and wrapped around someone else's finger.

"You're right," said Abigail. "I suppose they are just a nice gift."

"Well, when he does make himself known, it will be a conversation starter. That is, if he's amiable enough and will make an ideal husband for you," she giggled.

Abigail could only pay her a slight smile before retreating to her room, silk flowers in hand. The idea of ever meeting this admirer face to face sent chills down her spine. Whatever his game was, he ruined his chances by hurting Ian and sending his goons to scare her. But she'd prove that she wasn't afraid.

Without hesitation, she stood by her open window and tore away the seams that held the delicate silk together. It didn't matter if anyone saw her or not. But it proved something to herself. She wouldn't be toyed with. Not now, or ever.

Adam slumped against the cabin door, beyond exhausted and aware of his healing wound that had been throbbing constantly since they boarded. It was cleaned and stitched while Ian's nose was set back into place. Despite what they were given to numb the pain,

Adam could tell Ian shared the same complaining thoughts as he sat in the opposite corner with a bloodied rag over his face.

In the brig, Phillip sat against the iron bars on a makeshift bed, staring at the wall away from Adam's gaze. The room was small and dim, the only light coming from the grated ceiling hatch that beamed down upon Phillip's still form.

The men voted he'd stay there until he calmed down and his sanity returned. Adam opted to stay with him for the first few hours just to be sure he didn't hurt himself, and Ian agreed to watch Adam, lest he tore his stitches or fever set in from infection.

"We made it out alive," said Adam. "I couldn't have done it without you."

"Oh don't get all sappy on me now, Garrow. I'm already teary enough as it is," Ian said, joking about his broken nose.

"It hurts to laugh," Adam chuckled.

"Yeah, well it hurts to cry."

"We read and hear stories about men surviving adventures. I guess there's a reason they don't go into detail about the recovery time. It's long and tedious after being burned, beaten, shot at, and nearly stabbed to death."

"The same for being whipped," Ian said with a faraway look, but he changed the subject. "What about him? How will his recovery go?"

"We talk to him. He knows me, and he knows you. I remind him of his family . . . and you remind him of Iris."

Suddenly, Phillip's head turned as if it were a direct reaction to Adam's words.

"Phillip?" said Adam, but Phillip only looked back at the wall and remained silent.

Ian lowered the rag and raised his eyebrows. "He must have responded to her name."

"Quick, do you have any memories of her to describe to him?"

Ian concentrated, staring far away into the recesses of his mind. He hadn't spoken of the Westmont family since that day in Adam's parlor, and Adam never pressed it, but now was not the time to avoid stepping on eggshells.

Eventually Ian leaned forward, keeping a good distance but close enough for Phillip to hear better.

"Phillip . . . remember the day ya met Iris? Ya told me how ya ran her over in the street. Her smile was radiant and genuine when she looked at ya. She smelled of . . . rosewater and lilac. It was love at first sight. Ya said it was the moment she became your princess." It was hard to gauge whether Phillip was really listening as he continued to stare blankly at the wall. But then a single tear spilled over his cheek, and his lips parted to exhale a shaky breath.

Adam felt the hope well up inside him and was grateful to Iris Westmont for giving his brother something to hold onto. He already knew the powerful effect such a simple memory could have. And he was grateful for Ian to be around to share it.

For a minute, it reminded Adam of the day he met Solana. He had no idea where she was right now or if she had already moved on with someone else. But regardless, some memories are held onto just to get people through difficult times—even just through a hard day like this one.

But the following week had proven just as hard. Since they boarded, Adam was taken to his breaking point dealing with Phillip's fluctuating mood swings. It started with screaming rage mixed with loud sobbing. Occasionally they heard random laughter, but most of the time it was stunned silence.

But eventually his emotions quieted down, and most of the time he just sat still looking bored. Whether he wasn't capable or chose not to, Phillip didn't speak.

Ian theorized he wasn't being challenged enough, that he was dependent on getting what he needed without asking for it, so he didn't.

Adam wasn't sure he was ready to be pushed yet. But considering they'd be interacting with crowds of people soon, it looked like they didn't have much of a choice.

"What do we do when we dock in England?"

Adam sighed. "I don't think God would see us fail just yet. We'll figure it out as we go."

"What do ya think, Phillip?" asked Ian.

He looked up in Ian's direction but only blinked.

"Do ya even want to go home?" Phillip looked back down, and Ian let out a frustrated grunt. "It's time to let him out."

Adam's brows furrowed. "The door is open. We're not holding him here."

"He's bein' lazy."

"What is this attitude of yours?"

"What's this attitude of *yours*? Ya need to stop coddlin' him!"

"Oh, shut up!" exclaimed Phillip, standing and sulking out of the cabin like an annoyed adolescent.

Ian and Adam sat motionless for a minute and then looked at each other.

"Who knew bickering like an old couple would get him to say his first words?" said Adam.

Ian shrugged. "Livin' with my family . . . sounds about right."

Adam snorted and gingerly stood up, holding his still tender side. Leaving the cabin, they both didn't have to look very long to find Phillip leaning against the railing, staring down into the choppy blue-green water.

Adam made his presence known before putting a hand on Phillip's shoulder, but he wrenched out of his grasp. "Leave me alone," he grumbled.

"Phillip—"

"No! They've been fighting all morning, and it's your fault because you left us!"

Adam took a step back, eyeing his brother questioningly. "Who's been fighting?"

"Mama cannot sleep . . . Papa is never home . . . and no matter what I do, it never makes up for your loss."

"What's he talkin' about?" asked Ian.

"I have no idea," Adam said. "Could be another mental break."

"Do we snap him out of it?"

Adam shook his head. "Let's play it out. I have a feeling this will happen a lot until it's out of his system."

Phillip paced the deck, muttering to himself. Occasionally he sat down, rubbing his knees until they became raw. And then he'd pace again, starting the process all over. When Adam tried approaching him, he made the mistake of putting a hand on Phillip's shoulder, and Phillip's fist met his jaw.

When the shores of England at last came into view, Adam went into the cabin and found Ian reading a book while Phillip sat on a crate, braiding a piece of rope. He was finally doing something productive, and Adam wondered just how lucid he was.

"What's he doing?" Adam asked Ian.

It was Phillip who answered. "What does it look like?"

Ian lowered the book and looked at him with a proud smile. "He's awake," he said.

"Phillip?"

"Yes?" he answered.

"Please don't be messing with me."

Phillip chuckled and stood, opening his arms so Adam could embrace him as much as he could with a sore torso.

"How long have you been lucid?"

"About an hour," said Phillip. "I don't know how long it'll last, but I feel pretty calm right now."

Adam looked at Ian, who still remained seated, pretending to flip the pages. "Why didn't you fetch me sooner?"

"Well as much as I enjoyed watchin' ya get beat up, I had to be sure it wasn't a false alarm."

"About that, Adam, I'm sorry for lashing out so violently," said Phillip remorsefully. "Majority of the time, I wasn't aware of where I was or who I was really with."

Adam raised a hand. "It was nothing. I probably deserved most of it."

"All right, before it gets too mushy," said Ian, tossing the book while he stood, "we're almost to the coast, Phillip is out of the woods of insanity . . . at least we hope so, and we have no plan. On the island, Melgar's first mate told us Phillip had been sold. Who would sell ya?"

"Someone who thought Melgar would kill me," said Phillip. "They didn't anticipate Adam coming after me."

"Then who would want ya dead?"

Phillip's teeth gritted. "Someone wanting complete control of my accounts and all the shares I have."

"Could ya just return home and take it back?"

"Maybe," said Adam, "but it leaves Phillip exposed. Whoever wanted him gone just might go after Phillip again."

"Well, we've made it this far, haven't we?" Ian stated. "And Phillip, would you really let that stop you from coming home to Iris?"

Phillip pinched the bridge of his nose. "She probably thinks I'm dead."

"Then all the better she'll feel when she sees ya alive." Ian then pointed to Adam. "And ya got nothin' to lose."

"Except I'm no one's favorite person right now. And it doesn't help that I disappeared with one of Phillip's ships."

"They'll overlook it when they see ya a hero for bringin' Phillip home. That girl—Solana, I believe her name was—might give ya second chance."

Adam actually smiled at that logic. Despite everything they had gone through, apparently there was hope on the horizon.

"So the two of ya need to think. Where do ya go to wait out a storm?" Ian asked.

The three of them were silent until Phillip's expression brightened. "Burnheart," he said. "Adam, the land is still yours. We can at least go there to lay low until we discover who has control over my accounts."

"That's not a bad idea," said Adam. "That way we don't make a spectacle of ourselves, and we can expose the culprit with the element of surprise."

"It will take time."

"Then we'll use it wisely."

"Any chance either of you will need a stableman?" Ian asked.

Phillip scoffed. "Ian, I think it's safe to say you're a part of the family now. But with that being said, this is not your problem. We'd understand if you don't want to get involved in all this."

"I didn't risk me life savin' your hide to let ya get yourself tangled up again. And this is the closest I've been to bein' a part of a family since mine were killed."

"Well, then I suppose that's it," said Adam. "Let's go home and take back what's ours."

When their ship docked, the vessel was thoroughly searched by town officials, and the crew was questioned for their intentions. Ian surprised them when his Irish accent disappeared as he was addressed by an official on the docks.

"Good day," Ian said, putting on a charming persona as he proffered his hand.

The official accepted it and gave a curt nod. "Good day. Your reason for visit, sir?"

"I'm traveling with these brutes," he joked.

"His cousins," Phillip added, to make his reasoning stronger.

Ian nodded. "It's good to be home. Nothing beats the scenery after weeks spent staring at vast ocean."

"Indeed," the official said. "Well, you gentlemen best be on your way then."

"Thank you, sir. As well as for your service." Ian bowed his head and followed them nonchalantly down the harbor.

"What was that?" exclaimed Adam in a low voice.

"Learned that trick on the way here," he answered in his normal Irish brogue. "Didn't want to seem out of place with you lot. And I didn't think I'd be this happy to see England again."

"Never thought I *would* see this place again," Phillip added.

"If you both are done being sentimental . . . let's get out of here. We need to see what we missed."

And no doubt they missed a lot.

At the harbor's inn, Adam walked inside in search of Sam, the man who ran the establishment. Ian and Phillip went to the livery in hopes of purchasing a few good horses, as well as keeping Phillip out of sight.

"Can I help ya?" asked the innkeeper.

At first glance, he knew he'd be hard to recognize. His beard had grown in thick with hair grown past his ears. The grime he'd accumulated from the boat didn't help either.

"Sam, it's me."

He gave Adam a long, hard stare until he uttered, "Well I'll be darned. Look who's back in town!"

"Shhh," he said, chuckling. "I came to hear some town gossip. What did I miss?"

"What did ya miss? First off, where've ya been?"

"Surviving," Adam sighed, trying to keep it vague. "But can you tell me anything newsworthy that may have happened in the last few months?"

He shrugged. "None that would be interestin' to ya."

"Anything about the Westmont sisters?"

He perked up, knowing exactly where he was getting at. "That's right, one of them was engaged to Phillip!" He shook his head. "Those girls are rarely seen these days. Holed up with no interest in findin' husbands is what I hear. Men pass through here, grumblin' over too much pretty gone to waste."

Phillip will be happy to hear that, Adam thought. "I bet that Rosenlund girl is snatched up."

"Which one?"

"The oldest."

"Oh yes . . . her," he said, staring into space as if trying to remember. Adam tried to wait patiently for a response, but he was getting antsy. "She ain't married yet, but I heard she'll be gettin' engaged soon, if ya know what I mean."

Adam's stomach twisted. "Engaged to who?"

"Nothin' official, but that Deveraux boy, Camden, has been eyein' her for weeks. Just been too busy to properly court her, I guess, with tryin' to fix up . . ." he trailed off, and Adam could easily figure out by the grave look on his face what he planned to say next.

"He took over Phillip's estate . . . didn't he?"

"I'm sorry, Adam," he said again, genuine sympathy lacing his words.

Adam tried to remain calm but had to clench his jaw to do it. "It doesn't surprise me at all, actually. Thank you for your help."

"Anytime. Best of luck to ya."

Adam rushed to the livery, a million thoughts running through his head, until he found Ian looking over a horse he seemed interested in.

"Oh good, you're back," said Ian. "We only have enough for two horses, but it'll get us to a good place to set up a campsite if we need to."

"Fine," said Adam. "But I have good news and bad. Good news is I believe I already know who has hold of your shares. Bad news—it's Richard Deveraux."

Phillip cursed loudly as he took hold of his own hair into his fist. "Of course it's Richard Deveraux!"

"I take it he's the man we don't like," said Ian.

"He's a greedy, pompous vulture," said Phillip. "And I wouldn't be surprised if he had something to do with our whole family's demise."

"The fire as well?" Adam offered.

Phillip threw his hands in the hair. "Why not? What I wouldn't give to see the look on his face when he sees I'm alive."

"Well, we can't point fingers yet, but anyone who attempts to off an entire legacy usually has a dark history and leaves a paper trail behind. That's our next step."

"Could we afford to get a bit closer?" asked Ian.

"How would we go about that?"

"Well, I'm a nobody; he won't recognize me. Let's say there's a party he attends, and he gets a bit tipsy. I could sneak in and ask him a few questions."

Adam scowled. "It's risky."

"But an idea," said Phillip. "It's August now, but in a month or so, the Rosenlunds will be hosting their annual harvest party."

The three stood in silent contemplation, but they seemed resolved with what they planned to.

"Fine," said Adam, "but it will take a good distraction to get you inside, Ian. You're a nobody, but I don't have much to lose either. And you'll need backup if you're caught."

"We'll work something out," said Phillip. "But first, I need food, a haircut, and a good shave. Let's get to Burnheart."

$\mathscr{S}$EVENTEEN

— ❦ —

$\mathscr{S}$olana walked out into the courtyard, breathing in the late summer night air that brought back a wave of nostalgia. Though the Rosenlunds' apples weren't their main source of living, the fall harvest was widely celebrated. Every year, the Rosenlund family threw a party in the courtyard of their home for all the tenants, friends, and employers.

Dozens of parchment paper lanterns hung on string that crossed overhead. The tables were adorned with bouquets of roses and wildflowers, along with trays of delicious food. Near the stone pond, musicians played their instruments, and the guests danced the traditional steps.

It wasn't as grand as the balls she'd attended during her season in London, but Solana preferred her family celebrations over anything else, especially when the laughter was genuine and the dancing more lively.

Solana fidgeted a little in her corset. Normally she wore something more casual on this occasion, but this year was different from others. She'd be twenty soon, and her parents were getting more determined than ever to find her a match, which required her to wear something that stood out amongst her other dresses.

"Solana!" called Faye, scurrying toward her as fast as she could in her new slippers. She always complained about how they pinched her toes, but her stubbornness won out when she decided they were too pretty to give away.

"Yes?"

She giggled. "The Deverauxs are here!"

Solana frowned. "Already?"

"Why don't you look happy? We'll get to see Camden."

Solana could see why Faye would become dreamy-eyed in his presence, but she didn't have much interest when it came to his attitude or his looks. And she hated the idea of what her parents were likely planning for them tonight. Camden and her father had become too close for comfort these days.

"Faye, I think your friend Collette has arrived."

Faye rolled her eyes, understanding she was being dismissed, but left without a retort. Watching her leave, Solana meandered through the crowd of people, keeping herself occupied with other guests before her father could drag her away.

But amidst the swarm of conversing visitors, a lone figure caught her eye.

He was leaning against the farthest wall, wearing dark trousers, a black vest, and a white shirt.

His hair was akin to mahogany, styled nicely but cropped short enough to just touch his brow, and his chin sported a few days' scruff. But what really stood out was that he donned a black mask that covered only the upper half of his face, tying around with leather straps.

This party wasn't a masquerade, nor could she think of anyone eccentric enough to show up dressed in such a way. He was talking to no one, merely observing, before his hard gaze met hers.

Solana froze, unconsciously trapped in his stare, and could have sworn she saw the curve of his mouth twitch into a smile. But as soon as a striding couple blocked her vision, he disappeared.

"What . . . ?" she breathed, pushing through the crowd to see where he ran off to, but her attention was averted when she caught sight of her two favorite people in the world.

With her spirits lifted, she rushed up behind them and feigned nonchalance as she said, "Well look at the splendors that finally decided to show."

Both Westmont sisters turned around, and all three squealed with excitement upon seeing each other. With a firm embrace, Abigail was the first to gush over Solana's appearance.

"Just look at you," she exclaimed. "You appear like a lady who just stepped out of your mother's book of propriety."

"Should I take that as a compliment?"

"You look beautiful," Iris added.

"Thank you. I can't believe you made it, Iris. After what happened to Phillip—"

"I'm still in shock," Iris cut off. "But until I receive an official letter that he's . . . not coming back, I'll press on as normally I can. So tonight we will eat, dance, and be friends like we used to be."

"Then let's make it so," said Solana. "I've missed you. Will you both be staying through the weekend?"

"We hope so," said Abigail. "But like all things with Papa, nothing is ever final until the last minute."

"Well for my sake, I surely hope he considers it. How are you two enjoying the party? Anyone meet your fancy this year, Abby?"

Before she could answer, Solana felt a tap on her shoulder. Based on her friend's amused expressions before she turned around, she knew exactly who stood behind her.

Instinctively, her nose wrinkled.

"Pardon me for interrupting, ladies," said Camden. "Hello, Miss Rosenlund. I was hoping you wouldn't mind stealing away a moment to walk with me."

Iris giggled, and Abigail gave her a reassuring smile as she answered for her. "Oh, she'd love to. We were just finished talking."

"Wonderful," he stated, holding out his elbow. She took it without much feeling and glanced back at her "friends" who were slyly waving her off. She stuck out her tongue and resolved to get them back for this.

"How have you fared these past months?" he asked. "I've been meaning to make better contact, but my father keeps me busy."

"I'm doing well, thank you," she answered plainly.

By now the musicians were playing, and Solana relied on the stringed instruments and flutes to drown out most of Camden's chatter. It was when he cleared his throat that she started paying attention.

"I'm sorry, what?" she said.

She didn't miss the flash of annoyance in his eyes before he repeated, "How do you feel about the new fashion trends I've seen in London? I was just thinking the other day that if you put a little more effort in staying current, you would consistently look stunning."

This wasn't the first time he attempted to compliment her while degrading her appearance in the process. She learned quickly to hide her "Are you being serious?" look and say, "Thank you," hoping to move on from the subject.

Thankfully, the music had changed and many were joining around the stone floor for a traditional dance she learned during her childhood. Placing her hands in his, she glanced around at the other couples as the music started at a steady pace. Many were watching her with grand expectations, and she put on the most pleasant facade for their benefit.

But as Camden twirled her, keeping a distance, she could feel something missing. For the sake of her family and future, she wanted to like him. And for some reason, it seemed impossible when his presence took a toll on her energy more than anyone else.

It was about a minute into the dance when the music unexpectedly quickened in tempo, and all the couples stopped.

As if it were planned, all the musicians and hired help broke into a steady clap as the man wearing the black mask appeared by the southeast wall. Solana's gaze was at first captured by his feet as he stepped faster to the drums, making a sound equally as loud. It wasn't random, but rhythmic and entrancing.

Once the violas came in, he began to show off acrobatic moves, twisting in the air and walking on his hands. Solana continued to stare in awe and wonder. Iris and Abigail soon joined her and exchanged elated whispers. Camden seemed less than happy for the interruption.

Once more, the music changed slightly, keeping the fast rhythm but transitioning as he ran into the crowd. The man came closer and closer until he reached out and he seized Solana's waist. She let out a small gasp from the surprise as he took her hand and led her in a dance she had no choice but to go along with.

He pulled her close, and she held onto him. Her fear was not being held by a stranger, but if he were to let go, the force would send her flying off her feet!

Everyone cheered and clapped as he twirled her around the courtyard. For a moment, she glanced at the man's face. His brown eyes were distinctly familiar, but what caught her breath was his attention toward her. He looked nowhere else but at her, and his mouth turned up in a smile as heat rose in her cheeks—the blush likely becoming more visible to him.

Exhilaration curtly replaced all feeling as he lifted her into the air and gently placed her back on her feet. Again, she laughed out loud from enjoyment.

All too soon, the mysterious man took his cue and released her waist, throwing her out and pulling her back into his arms as the last note played.

The guests cheered, but all she could hear was her own beating heart and labored breathing.

Solana was still shocked, figuring he must have been hired entertainment, but it wasn't typical for her father—or anyone she knew—to do something against tradition. And her assumption was proven wrong when the guards hired to keep the riffraff away for the night started indignantly making their way toward him.

The stranger's gaze returned to Solana as he approached her. He reached down and brought her hand to his lips. He was still out of breath as he exhaled in a low voice, "My lady . . . until we meet again."

The man suddenly fled speedily through the crowd, scaling the far wall in one jump, disappearing into the night. The chatter and awe increased, but none of the visitors seemed to be disappointed with the performance.

As the adrenaline pulsed through Solana's veins, she made a quick glance over at Abigail and Iris. Back on solid ground, she began to giggle, but their bonding moment was soon broken when Solana's father and Camden stormed to her side.

"Are you all right?" her father asked frantically, grasping her shoulders and appraising her down from head to toe. She wasn't quite sure what he was looking for, but she pulled away from his grasp.

"I'm wonderful," she reassured. "A little out of breath, but that was the most enjoyment I've had in a long time."

"Yes, that was quite surprising," Camden mumbled, avoiding eye contact.

"Papa, why are you so upset? He didn't mean any harm."

Her father was generous and understanding in most cases, but when it came to the welfare of his family and estate, his temper and stubbornness almost always won over.

"Camden, would you excuse us for a moment?" he asked.

Camden gave them a curt nod and departed in silence, and Christopher looked down at Solana, lowering his voice into a harsh whisper. "He trespassed onto my property and touched my daughter without consent. Not only am I humiliated, but you just outright spoke down to the best possible suitor, expressing your enjoyment of being manhandled by a miscreant. What does that say about you? Certainly it says nothing about being a prospective wife!"

He spat the last word, which made Solana jump a little. Shame and fear were beginning to take over her feelings, and a quiet "I'm sorry" was all she could say.

"You should go inside," he said.

"But Papa, the party just started!"

"Do not argue with me. I can get Camden to escort you back to the house."

"No," she retorted defiantly.

"Solana, you will do as I say and not continue to argue with me about it."

"I do not need an escort," she mumbled, ripping herself away before he could reprimand her further.

Solana wasn't the kind to make a scene, but she wasn't going to let Camden, her father, or anyone ruin her night. Instead, she held her chin high and entered the house on her own. If she could have, she would've stayed for the party, but there was only so much defiance she could express before her father locked her away for the rest of the summer.

Upon entering the household, Solana forced him out of her head and relived the happier moments of the evening. The spontaneity and romantic notion of *literally* being swept off her feet was both scandalous and exhilarating, to say the least.

She went inside as she was told but made her way to the kitchen and exited the back door. Impulsively, she kept going until she reached the stables. Past it was the orchard, a place where she'd find more seclusion than within the walls of her own home, which was what she truly wanted right now.

With only the light of the moon to guide her through the trees, everything was basked in a silver glow. It was both enchanting and almost unnerving.

"You shouldn't be out here," a voice said, and she jumped, her hand flying to her chest.

She turned to see a tall figure leaning against an apple tree, arms folded, displaying an amused grin, and wearing a black mask.

$\mathcal{E}$IGHTEEN

$\mathcal{I}$an did his best to keep a low profile, but didn't have to work very hard when everyone's attention was drawn to the man in the mask. Now Ian understood why Adam asked for dance lessons. He had insisted on going big for the event, and Ian could only shake his head at the guts he had for pulling it off. At least it gave Ian the chance to scale the wall and make it into the courtyard without being detected.

Now Ian searched for the gentleman of the evening. Considering what Phillip described him to be, Ian spotted Richard Deveraux next to the champagne table. His face was flushed, and he had just emptied his glass to pick up a new one.

Now was Ian's chance.

In his best English accent, Ian approached him and said, "Pardon me, sir. I couldn't help but notice you are the famous Mr. Deveraux, the man who revived the Fairbrooke estate."

"Indeed, I am!" he said a bit too loudly. "And who might you be?"

"An admirer of yours. I'd very much like to know how you pulled off such a feat."

"Blood, sweat, and tears," he said with a wide grin, and then he leaned in to whisper, "Most of it not from myself."

"Intriguing," said Ian, trying not to gag from his rancid breath. "Who else would give their blood, sweat, and tears on your behalf?"

"My son, for starters. God bless that boy. But you know who else?" He looked up toward the sky for a moment and then shrugged with a hearty laugh. "I forget."

Ian fought the urge to roll his eyes. "I'm sure Phillip Garrow would appreciate what you've done on his behalf."

"I'm sure he would, indeed. Though the lad got what was coming to him."

"Did he?"

"Oh yes. Just like his father did," he said, gazing blankly off into the distance. Now they were getting somewhere.

"What about his father?"

"Some people are just destined to burn. Excuse me," Richard said, quickly putting down his glass down and pushing his way into the crowd.

Ian attempted to follow him, but in the distance, the familiar color of sun-kissed auburn hair caught his attention. For a moment, he stood frozen in place, fixated on the woman who broke his heart. He should've expected to see Abigail here. He'd never seen her so dressed up for a party before. But even from a distance, he could picture how much her green dress would bring out her eyes.

When her face turned his direction, Ian felt his stomach jolt. He wasn't supposed to be recognized, and his heart raced father when she moved in his direction.

Thinking quickly, Ian fled around the tables and into the open entrance. He maneuvered through the corridor, dodging trays and sidestepping guests, until he found an empty room with a window. Unlocking the hatch, he lifted the frame and ungracefully tumbled out onto the lawn.

He felt like a fool for making such a ridiculous escape. But with the last of his dignity, he dusted off his trousers and made his way to the orchard to find the horses. He only hoped Adam was already waiting at their rendezvous point and hadn't gotten caught, because Ian was not in the mood for another rescue mission.

Solana backed away a little in precaution, but the masked man didn't move. "Who are you?" she asked.

"Someone who clearly wasn't supposed to be here tonight."

"Then why are you?"

"It's a long story," he said, chuckling.

"Did you wait here, expecting I'd follow you?"

"No, I'm waiting for a friend. Truthfully, I didn't think I'd ever see you again. But it's funny how we keep meeting like this."

She scowled. "Meeting like how?"

"It's a long story," he repeated, but this time with a heavy sigh. "You should get back to your party. They'll be missing you."

Solana didn't miss the slight frown when he said it. "No, I'd like to understand. Meeting like how?"

There was a long pause before he stood up straight. "Do I look familiar to you at all?"

Solana took a moment to give him a good look. It was hard to see particular features, but everything about him—his tall, lean physique and broad shoulders, his angular jaw and dark hair—seemed familiar, but only to an extent.

"It's hard to answer in this light."

Leaning down, he picked up a lantern and scratched flint against steel. Something about seeing the spark unnerved her. She wasn't sure why, but it triggered a memory of watching someone striking flint and herself not reacting well to it.

But all the man did was light the lantern and hold it near his face. The soft glow illuminated his features a bit more as he reached back to untie the strings that held his mask to his face.

Seeing the complete picture, Solana's breath caught. She *had* seen this man before. The way the light danced against his features, his searching eyes fixated completely on her—it took Solana back to a single moment. It felt so brief but had significant meaning.

"You were there," she whispered. "The day of the fire."

"Yes."

"You carried me away from the flames," she said, remembering the smoke-filled sky and being in his arms.

"I did."

But she also remembered his face in a different setting. His face was sad, and it rained heavily. "And you were at the funeral."

"I was."

"And now you're here."

"I am."

"Why?" she asked. "Who are you?"

He took one step closer to her, holding one hand up in reassurance. "You know me, Solana."

She shook her head in frustration. "Please just tell me who you are. If you mean something to me, I want to know."

Right then, the sound of a horse whinnied in the distance. "Perfect timing as usual," he said, but it sounded sarcastic enough to make her worry.

"Are you in trouble?"

"No, he's just my ride home. Which means I have little time to explain anything further, but . . . we *will* see each other again."

He reached out as if to touch her cheek, but then he retracted, looking disappointed that he couldn't. Still, he was close enough for her to smell oak, tanned leather, burnt cedar, and citrus. It brought her back, not to a memory, but to one of her dreams. Her fantasy of walking through the orchard with a man that held her complete attention *and* affection.

Too soon, two horses emerged between the rows of trees. One had a cloaked rider, but the other carried an empty saddle.

"I have to go," he sighed, holding out the lantern for her to take. "One day I'll find you again. Get home safely."

Solana's heart beat quickly as the man took off toward the horse. The horse slowed down, but only enough for the man to agilely jump onto the saddle. He snapped the reins and the two sped away in full stride into the night.

Solana dared not blink. He promised they would see each other again. But when would that be? And under what circumstances?

There was one thing she did know: this man was no stranger to her. And if he'd been involved in rescuing her from the fire, there was something her parents had left out of their story. Whatever it was, Solana was ready for the truth.

With everyone distracted by the merriment, Solana conspicuously snuck back into the house through the kitchen door.

She rushed to her bedroom and closed the door quietly, believing she'd be alone. But her heart skipped when she turned and found both Abigail and Iris waiting for her.

"You near scared the life out of me!" she squealed. "What are you two doing here?"

Abigail was the first to speak as she lounged on the coverlet, flipping through one of her books. "Where have you been?"

"The orchard perhaps?" Iris suggested.

Solana let out an exasperated sigh. "Is that so unusual?"

"Oh, come off it, Solana. You know you can't hide anything from us—certainly not from me," said Abigail.

"Who were you with?" asked Iris.

Solana feigned ignorance. "I wasn't with anyone."

Iris tilted her head. "You mean to say you didn't sneak off to meet that masked gentleman in the orchard?"

"That the whole performance wasn't rehearsed?" Abigail added.

Solana raised her chin. "Of course not. I have no reason to keep secrets from either of you. This whole evening has been just as surprising for me as it was for you two. However . . . you're right, I wasn't in the orchard alone. I found him there."

"The masked gentleman?" asked Iris.

Abigail rolled her eyes. "Naturally."

"And yes, somehow I *do* know him." Their eyes narrowed, and Solana continued. "I remember the fire. Not everything, but a short moment when he carried me out of the flames."

Iris let out a small gasp, but it was Abigail who asked, "Are you certain it wasn't your imagination?"

"Positive," she said firmly. "I can't remember before or beyond that moment, but it was real."

"Do you know his name?"

"He left before he could tell me. A figure in a dark cloak came riding up, and they left together."

Abigail gazed intently into space, deep in thought. "Why would he interrupt a party and dance with you so brazenly in front of everyone?"

Solana laughed at herself. "I didn't think to ask. Either way, it was worth the experience. I don't think Camden could ever sweep me off my feet like that."

"He probably fancies you," Iris sighed.

"Then why would he leave? He was waiting for his getaway horse," said Solana. "I couldn't have been the only reason."

Abigail rolled her eyes. "Or he was just looking to disturb the peace and take advantage of a starry-eyed young woman."

Solana almost leaned back from her sudden change in demeanor. "Excuse me?"

"He did treat you rather *familiarly* in public, Solana. And you never said anything about giving him permission in the first place. Regardless, you did so without knowing who this man was. What does that say about you? Do you have any idea how improper that was your part?"

"Abby, you know me better than that," Solana defended.

"You went into the orchards alone."

"I already told you I did not plan to meet him there."

"It was still reckless," Abigail scolded.

Solana was hurt at what Abigail was implying. "Are you suggesting that I have little regard for my innocence?"

"Of course not, but you could use more discretion in your actions. I only worry for your well-being. I'd hate to see you end up heartbroken or . . . compromised."

As much as Solana didn't want to admit it, they were right to be worried. But because they weren't there, neither could understand it all fully.

"You two should go back to the party," said Solana. Iris reached for Solana's hand, but she pulled away. "I appreciate your regard for my well-being. But I'm a grown woman, and you don't know what it's like to have a piece of your life missing. A piece you want to remember but can't, until a stranger shows up with part of the answer."

Abigail pursed her lips. "You're right. But I do know what's it's like to have a stranger show up and take something away from me."

After Abigail stormed out of the room, Solana gave Iris an inquisitive look. "She used to not be like this. What happened to her?"

Iris's shoulders slumped. "We haven't spoken much recently. At first I couldn't, after she gave me the letter about Phillip. But she's far too jumpy and short-tempered. She *has* changed, but there's something she's keeping to herself."

"Her and everyone else, it would seem."

NINETEEN

Arriving at Burnheart, Adam unsaddled his horse and joined Phillip next to the fire pit he set up outside.

"Please tell me that ridiculous plan of yours was a success," said Phillip.

"On my end, it was," Adam said, chuckling. "Though I may have stirred the pot a little, which can be either good or bad."

"Stirred the pot how?"

"I saw Solana dancing with Camden, and I couldn't resist stealing her away from him. The look on his face was worth it, but her father wasn't very happy. And she later found me waiting for Ian in the orchard."

"Did anyone recognize you? Did *she* recognize you?"

"I don't think so. And not entirely."

Phillip pinched the bridge of his nose. "Adam, why do you always have to make a show of everything?"

Adam's eyes widened. "A show?"

"You act far too impulsively for your own good."

"My impulsive actions are what brought you home."

"And as grateful as I am for that, I just . . ." he trailed off, wincing as though in pain. He then put his head into his hands, taking slow, even breaths, and Adam realized what he was seeing.

In the course of just a few months, Phillip went from faultless younger brother to weathered-down leader. And after hiding away his insecurities, putting on a brave front in the face of danger, and losing most of what he loved, it didn't surprise Adam to see Phillip's weaknesses starting to show.

"You're scared," said Adam.

"I'm scared," he confirmed. "I'm vulnerable, I feel powerless, I miss Iris . . . and I miss our parents."

A tear spilled down Phillip's cheek, and Adam placed a hand his shoulder. "You're human, Phillip. I miss them too, every day."

"I know. I just wish they were here to tell me what to do."

"They do," said Ian, moving to join their circle. "Ya just have to listen more carefully."

Phillip nodded in agreement but changed the subject by asking, "Did you find Deveraux?"

"I did. Of course he didn't give me any solid information, but he did say something about your father. That he got what was coming to him. That he was destined to *burn*."

Phillip's eyes hardened. "That's all I needed to know. Adam, you and I will visit the solicitor tomorrow. We'll stay discreet, but I think we have enough motive to start investigating."

"What about Iris?" Ian asked. "Do ya want her to know you're alive?"

"Not yet. If Richard somehow discovers I'm onto him, he could get to me through her."

"Bummer."

"Yes," Adam agreed. "But at least we have each other."

Phillip snorted. "Don't depress me further."

Ian laughed at that, and Adam joined in, finding it better than sulking in their problems.

"Well, in case you were wonderin'," said Ian. "Iris was at the party, and she looked fetchin' as ever."

Phillip smiled at that. "Did you see Abigail there as well?"

"Um, no. Didn't get the chance to."

"Oh come off it. I bet you couldn't resist a quick glance."

"Phillip, I wouldn't," said Adam.

Ian stood quickly and pulled the hatchet embedded in a nearby stump. "I'm gettin' more firewood," he said before storming off to the woodpile.

"Clearly, I missed a few things while I was gone," said Phillip.

Adam's shoulders slumped. "You have no idea."

Cedric Westmont searched every room of Christopher's home until he found Iris sitting tensely in the library armchair.

"There you are," he said. "Would you care to join us for breakfast?"

Her smile was forced as she said, "In a minute, Papa."

With a nod and sympathetic look, Cedric proceeded to the dining room, where Christopher was seated at the head of the table.

They shook hands, and Cedric paid a small nod to his wife and daughters, who conversed quietly at the other end of the table.

"And what is your family conspiring about today, Chris?" he asked, smiling at how often the women plotted rather than planned. And it was apparent something was being concocted earlier in the day than usual.

"I'm always too afraid to find out," he answered.

"Is Iris coming?" asked Abigail, who came bounding in with her mother, Deirdre, and quickly joined the circle.

"She said she would be here soon, which is progress at least," said Cedric.

Deirdre nodded. "She's been wrapped in a better mood lately. Talking to people and more pleasant to be around."

Solana's eyes lit up suddenly, and she quickly turned to her father with a look of pleading. "Papa, I know this is a lot to ask, seeing it's a bit last-minute. But would you consider letting Abigail and Iris stay again for the rest of summer?"

Cedric nearly choked on his pastry. "Excuse me?"

"I mean no disrespect to you, sir, but at this time I only wish to have my most faithful friends here with me. There is a lot to think about with the Deveraux situation, and their advice and company would aid me greatly."

Christopher spoke then. "Our home is always welcome to them, Cedric."

Cedric scowled, every discouraging thought crossing his mind at the thought of leaving his children behind. But after they had arrived, Iris had never smiled more in one day than she did during that entire month.

"Solana, Iris, would you both excuse us for a moment?" Deirdre asked, sending a look to Cedric that indicated she was thinking the same thing. "There are a few things we need to discuss in private."

Without objection, they politely stood up and speedily exited the room with their breakfast plates.

"Arietta," Christopher called. "Would you see these young ladies to the kitchen? I do not particularly favor eavesdroppers."

The sounds of their frustrated sighs could be heard down the hallway, and their mothers were the ones to chuckle in amusement by it.

Once they were safely out of earshot, Margaret spoke first. "Cedric, I'd like to second my daughter's request." Suddenly, all were aware of the female conversation that had ensued earlier. "We all know how *spirited* Solana can be, and it's come to our attention that she will be facing a certain decision here soon."

Christopher cleared his throat. "Camden has hinted about a likely proposal of marriage, despite last night's events. Although she will always honor our wishes, she needs as much support as possible to willingly accept him. She seems very conflicted, and I believe it would do her good to have respectable friends nearby."

"And," Deirdre chimed in, "Iris could use a distraction from pining over Phillip. This may be a start to her finding some inner peace amongst people we consider to be family. And if Solana does marry Camden, this may encourage Abigail to seek out a suitor herself. I don't know what's gotten into that girl, but she received a beautiful silk rose hair piece from an admirer, and I found it torn apart in the rubbish."

Iris leaned against the dining hall doors, tears threatening to escape as she listened to her mother talk about her and Abigail that way.

She wasn't wrong, but it was clear to Iris that her mother didn't understand what she was going through. Neither did she with Abigail. And Iris couldn't blame her. They hadn't been easy to live with lately, and Iris did like the notion of being amongst good company, if only as a distraction.

She also found it humorous that Solana's parents would think her influence could convince the most stubborn of women to choose a man like Camden Deveraux.

She stifled a giggle just picturing it. Solana constantly rolling her eyes at his presence—snapping at his proper remarks—wincing at the thought of wearing a large, billowing, suffocating dress in front of a crowd . . .

There was no way Solana would make it that far without screaming in frustration. There was no way Abigail would be encouraged to marry either. If she were to stay, it would only give her the opportunity to provide her parents with the dissatisfaction of the opposite outcome.

Pulling herself together, Iris straightened out her dress, smoothed back her hair, and confidently marched into the dining room. Everyone's eyes were directed at her.

She looked to her mother, who gave her a welcoming smile. "Hello, darling. Did you sleep well?"

"Quite," she said, sitting down in the empty chair next to her father. She took notice of their searching looks and decided to take the opportunity to convince them of her pleasant nature in the Rosenlund home. "I'm much better rested than usual. I haven't had a decent night's sleep in ages."

Cedric wasted no time in recounting their discussion. "My dear, is it all right if I speak freely amongst company?"

"Of course, Papa. You can always speak freely, especially in front of such dear friends."

He grinned at her. "I miss that."

"You miss what?"

"Your smile. It's ever more present than I've seen in a long time."

Guilt once again washed over her. *Do I really wear such a permanent frown?* "I wasn't aware you could see a difference."

"Well, answer me honestly: are you happy here?"

"Of course I am. So many good memories linger here, and I love seeing Solana. I love the whole Rosenlund family," she said. "This place has a very . . . calming effect on me."

Everyone seemed to be silently voting over the decision, and then Margaret finally spoke. "Iris, would you and Abigail like to stay with us for the rest of summer?"

She raised her eyebrows, feigning surprise, and looked to her father. "Really? Is this what you have been discussing?"

"I was reluctant at first, I'll admit," Cedric answered. "After all, I was looking forward to having your company this summer. However, we would like to give you the option of staying here if that is your wish."

"And we'd love to have you," said Margaret. "It wouldn't be the same without the Westmont sisters with us."

"I'd love to stay," she said with no hesitation.

"When we return home, I'll have your belongings sent to you," said Deirdre, tears brimming in her lovely eyes, her smile never fading.

"Mama, if you don't wish this, I don't have to—"

"No, this is where you should be. Once you're finished eating, you should tell Solana and Abigail the good news."

Iris gave them a genuine smile and left at once, enjoying the way it made her feel. Perhaps there was something to hope for this summer after all. But the season had only just started, and anything could happen.

$\mathcal{T}$WENTY

---❧---

$\mathcal{T}$hree weeks passed since the night of the party, and Solana was growing restless.

As usual, Solana walked along the orchard, barefooted and in her casual attire. In a shadier region, she reached a small clearing that marked the border of the land.

Walking gave her clarity, and she was beginning to believe her friends were right in their assumptions—that the man in the mask would never return as he had promised. If only she knew his name or had some kind of evidence to keep her hopes up. But her expectations were beginning to dwindle.

Lately, her mother had been coaxing her into appearing in the brighter, fancier dresses that were brought to the front of her wardrobe. She could easily see the strategy behind it, for every time she appeared in public, Camden was always around to notice her. And he certainly did notice.

He'd always approach with a constant chatter that sent Solana's mind reeling. But whenever she was in his presence, she kept noticing him look her over from head to toe like a prized show horse. It always unsettled her, and she expected he'd do the same thing tonight at the dinner her parents invited him to.

Seeing how prestigious the dining room was being set to look, Solana expected Camden was planning to secure an engagement.

With all that he had to offer, and his ability to take care of her family's estate, how could she possibly say no to him?

She thought of what it would be like to be kissed by him, and an unexpected shiver crawled down her spine. She couldn't quite put her finger on it, but something about his presence didn't feel right to her.

Frustrated, she remembered why she came out here in the first place—to find peace and clarity—but it seemed too far out of reach. As fatigued as she was, her mind refused to settle down.

"Five minutes," she said out loud. "That's all I need, Lord. Five minutes with peace of mind."

As her words carried through the wind, Solana closed her eyes and took out the pins that held her hair so tightly to her head.

She inhaled deeply the scents that lingered in the grove. The perfumes of nature created images of trees, tall grasses, peculiar birds, and a small brook. Eventually she dozed off, those images slowly changing as her mind took control.

She could feel her body in the grass, but the sky was too dark for her to see anything. It wasn't night, but there was darkness. Suddenly the air became thick with a burning cloud that choked her lungs. Her head swam as the fumes intensified, removing her vision completely. A mess of noises roared through her ears, and she couldn't distinguish any of their sources.

But there was his face. It started from a shadow and then grew clearer until his features were brought into the light. She could even hear his voice, too, as he exhaled the words, "Thank the Lord," before bestowing a hard, driven kiss that startled her awake.

Solana bolted upright. She blinked from the light of the sun that now hung below the trees. Tears came to her eyes as she realized that she wasn't dreaming, but *remembering*.

It was slowly coming together, piece by piece. The scent, his touch . . . his name.

His name. She knew it.

Solana sprung to her feet and rushed back to the house. A missing piece had revealed itself, and what she remembered changed everything. How could she forget such a significant, life-altering moment?

Breathless, she reached the back entrance of the kitchen and burst through the door. Arietta jumped back in surprise, her flour-covered hand flying to her heart.

"Goodness, you frightened the wits out of me. What has you so frantic?"

"Do you know where my father is?" she panted, out of breath.

"He's upstairs. He asked not to be bothered, but if this is urgent . . ."

Solana could see the worry in the sweet woman's eyes. And something told her that Arietta perhaps knew the complete story.

"Arietta . . . if I asked you a question, would you answer me honestly?"

"Go on."

"That fire I was injured in . . . Was there anyone with Phillip when he brought me out of the flames?"

"Why do you ask?" she said, returning to her task of kneading bread dough, eyes now concentrated on *it* instead of her.

"I remember someone."

She paused. "Who do you remember?"

Her reaction was not one of confusion but of surprise, and Solana grew suspicious that Arietta was intentionally keeping something from her.

"Please answer the question," Solana pled. "Was there someone else?"

Arietta sighed, hanging her head low, conflicted in what she was about to say until she looked at Solana. "There is speculation that someone was on the property that day and started the fire on purpose."

It wasn't the answer Solana expected, but nonetheless, she was upset. "And no one thought to tell me this?"

"It's not my place to say. I don't blame anyone. The day was hot, and the fields were dry. Nature has its effect."

"Why would everyone keep this from me?" she asked.

"There are some things we experience in this world that we are blessed to keep as memories. And there are dark moments that can haunt us forever, and sometimes they can tear at a being's very soul if they let them. Be thankful you never have to be the one who must relive that dreadful day if that's all that you can remember."

"But there's something missing, Arietta!" she exclaimed. "And I need to know what it is. If there is a chance that something will evoke my memories of the rest of the story, I'd rather not let the trauma of it cause me to believe something false. I want to better understand so I won't go mad with wonder. *That* will tear at my soul."

Arietta sighed once more before she cleaned off her hands and sat down on a nearby stool. "That day no one could find you. You ran off somewhere like you usually do, and no one noticed your absence until your father left to assist while your mother stayed with Faye. As soon as he was with Caleb Garrow, someone had already been sent to fetch an unconscious young woman trapped behind the flames."

"Me."

She nodded. "And it was Caleb's son who immediately jumped through the smoke to retrieve you." Arietta put a hand to her heart. "Never had anyone seen a man run into the flames and not think twice about it. What a brave soul he was for saving you the way he did."

Solana's stomach sank. She remembered the Garrow family. Everyone did, but no one ever talked about them, at least never to her. But what disturbed her most was hearing of the man who saved her.

"You mean to tell me that it was just Phillip Garrow who saved me?" she asked.

"Indeed, it was. It is a real tragedy what happened to him after the bravery he displayed."

An endless string of questions now ran through her head. "What of the rest of the family?"

"You already know what happened to Lynnette."

"And their other children?"

"There were no other children. That's why the property and everything was taken over by the Deverauxs."

Solana slumped against the table, feeling deflated. Either Arietta was misinformed or Solana was hearing a doctored story. Phillip was certainly not the man she saw in her dream, and he wasn't an only child. He had a brother, who was definitely still alive.

"How is it that I don't remember all this?"

"The day you were found . . . you had lost your breath. Then you slipped back into unconsciousness and slept for two days. We were so worried that you wouldn't wake, or that you would pass on by means of starvation or thirst. But when you did come to, you couldn't tell us what happened. You acted as if you had woken up after a restful night's sleep. We had planned to explain everything in full detail, but you were still very weak—"

Solana couldn't discern which emotion was the strongest. She was angry for not having been told the fate of the Garrow family. She was mournful for everything they had lost, including their lives. And she was discouraged, knowing that despite what Arietta knew to be the truth, her main question still hadn't been answered.

Yes, she was now aware of the event that took place, but Phillip's brother played a role somehow, and the mystery still remained.

"Thank you," she forced herself to say. "I know that was difficult to reveal."

Arietta smiled timidly. "I'm sorry to have put this on your shoulders."

"There's no need to apologize."

Solemnly, she walked out of the kitchen, toward the staircase. As she began to ascend, she sat down on the stone steps and silently wept. She hated getting emotional, but it was too much to bear, remembering something so traumatic yet relieving at the same time.

After spending a few private moments weeping, she stopped feeling sorry for herself and wiped away the moisture, bravely continuing her determination. She was making progress, but like every puzzle, there's always a missing piece to search for.

In the drawing room, Solana found Iris sketching on a scrap parchment with a bit of charcoal. They never spoke about Phillip, and as much as she hated the idea of bringing back feelings of pain, it needed to be done.

Iris looked up and smiled. "Hello. Where have you been all day?"

"Finding some peace and quiet," Solana said truthfully.

"Doesn't surprise me. Mr. Deveraux and his family will be here soon."

"Listen," she said, changing the subject, "I came to address something, and I hope you won't take offense for what I'm about to ask."

Immediately Iris put down her utensils and brushed off her hands. "Go ahead."

"Did . . . did Phillip ever talk to you about that fire on his land?"

"Briefly. Why do you ask?"

Solana retold everything Arietta had shared with her; all the while Iris sat there speechless, apparently learning this story for the first time. As soon as she mentioned Phillip being the one who saved her, Iris became defensive.

"Phillip never mentioned this to me," she said, wrapping her arms around herself. "Why would he keep something like pulling you out of the flames from me?"

"Because he didn't," Solana told her. "His brother did."

"His brother is nowhere to be found."

"He was there, Iris. I remember him saying the name Adam."

"Could it have been someone else?"

"I know his face, Iris. Both he and the masked man are the same person."

Iris stood with gasp. "Are you sure?"

"Never have I been more certain in my life."

"If that's the case, he might know something about Phillip."

"Let's not get ahead of ourselves. We don't know Adam's place just yet, but he did say he planned to see me again."

Iris began wringing her hands as paced the floor. "You said there was a cloaked rider. It could have been Phillip."

Solana could see Iris was spiraling, and she stepped in front of her, placing both hands on Iris's shoulders. "Breathe, Iris. We don't know anything yet. But I will tell you when I do."

Solana wanted to feel confident in her reassurance, but her own questions of why Adam came back still hung in the air. Just how involved was he in the incident if he fled right after? Did something happen to him, or did he flee for a reason?

"There has to be more," Iris whispered. "If you remembered something, then more will come back to you.

"For all our sakes, I hope it does. I'm curious what Abigail will have to say about this. Do you know where she is?"

"The pond, I believe. It seems to be her place to go when she takes her daily walk."

"Shall we join her?"

"Might as well. I have too much energy, and I'd rather not be alone."

As Iris took Solana's invitation to leave, she left her sketches behind, all pleasant inspiration interrupted with the thought of Phillip.

Since the moment they met, he promised to make her laugh every day, and until his farewell, he kept that promise. Those happy memories were what kept his memory and her spirit alive. But now, after hearing what Solana described, she had her suspicions about the man she claimed to have seen the night of the fire.

She could understand why he didn't tell her more about it. As painful as it may have been, he wanted to marry her. If there was something he felt ashamed of, or enemies he might have had, she had the right to know. But she didn't doubt his character then, nor did she doubt him now.

Twenty-One

Abigail was more than happy to be away from her father's land. There, she couldn't help feeling watched or followed wherever she went. If a stable hand leered at her too long, she felt cold and empty inside. It provoked her to display a hardened indifference whenever she left the house, but it came across as shrewd behavior to her friends and family.

When she neared the tranquil pond, she sat on the grass and held her knees tight to her chest. Here, she could be in the fresh air without feeling the need to hide, and it allowed her space to concentrate on ridding her thoughts of Ian. No matter where she went, she saw his face in the crowd. Even at the party, he was vivid enough to for her to look twice.

"It wouldn't have worked," she said out loud. "He was a drifter with little means to provide. It was only a crush that meant nothing. Papa wouldn't have approved."

But that wasn't true. He was her friend, and talking to him had been the best part of her day. Instead of remembering his last cutting remarks, she couldn't stop herself from thinking about his laugh and the way he said her name so tenderly. She imagined what would've happened if they hadn't jumped apart before he had the chance to kiss her.

She'd gotten lost in that thought when the sound of a galloping horse broke her spell. She opened her eyes to see a rider in the distance coming toward the pond. He wore a coat and low cap that looked all too familiar.

Rising to her feet, she slowly made her way around the shallow beach. The rider dismounted, his face turned away as he patted the beast's neck. He hadn't noticed her approached him yet, but she was close enough to hear him say, "That's a good lass," and her breath caught.

She couldn't move. She even blinked a few times to make certain she wasn't hallucinating, but there he stood . . . Ian O'Connor.

Dumbfounded, she watched him shrug off his jacket and kneel at the pond's edge to splash water on his face. When he stood, he shook the water droplets form his hair. Abigail felt the blood rush back into her face.

"Ian?"

Hearing her, he turned around, and his expression mirrored hers. He looked scruffier than before, his facial hair growing into a trim beard that suited him. His nose appeared more crooked than she remembered, but it didn't detract from his handsomeness.

She couldn't believe that he was actually standing before her, but she knew her imagination couldn't have come up with this. This was real. But, as valid as it seemed, she couldn't release herself from her dreamlike state.

"Abigail?" he said, walking toward her. She contemplated backing away, but her legs wouldn't obey.

He moved in as if to give her hug, and instinctively, Abigail fisted her hand and punched him straight into his lower abdomen. He instantly doubled over with a grunt, resting his hands on his knees to brace himself.

"Oh dear," she choked, staring at her own hand in surprise.

Hitting him had never been a part of her fantasies at all. It was a knee-jerk reaction that came after being manhandled.

He didn't look up. She could barely hear him as he mumbled the words, "Ya *are* real."

"As are you," she said.

He raised himself up then. "Blimey! What was that for?"

"I didn't give you permission to come near me," she said quickly. It was the first reason that came to mind. "What were you expecting?"

"Not a punch to the gut," he grunted. "But I should have expected it after ya takin' me heart for the mill grinder."

He was right to assume that, but his presence still confused her. "How in the world are you here? Why are you on this property?"

"Valid questions."

"Are you going to answer them?"

"No."

She glared at him.

"I don't answer to ya anymore, lass. I stopped answerin' to ya the day ya sent me off," he said, turning toward the water's edge.

"You're the one to talk."

He stopped, looking back at her. "Me?"

"Yes, you."

"Are you accusin' me of somethin'? Enlighten me, princess. What exactly did I do to truly anger ya to the point of throwin' a punch? Because I can remember kneelin' on your father's land, stripped of me pride, accused of soilin' his daughter under a whip. But I took it. I submitted to such pain then, so I beg ya . . . what is the purpose of me submittin' to this pain right now?"

Abigail tried to speak, but none of the words that floated through her mind could form an audible sentence. The memories of that day were as fresh as the night she saw it all with her own eyes. But under his scrutinizing gaze, she had difficulty answering his question.

"Ya don't look surprised," he said suddenly, pulling her back to the moment.

She wasn't. She knew everything about the night he was bound and lashed. Of course, he didn't know that, but now she concluded that a real explanation of what they actually sacrificed that day would decrease the thickening tension.

"I know about the lashings," she said. "And I knew it had something to do with me. I didn't want you getting yourself killed—"

"So ya pushed me to leave," he finished.

She looked down, exhaling heavily. "I didn't think you would respond so angrily."

"Ya thought I'd be cheery about it?" he exclaimed, folding his arms across his chest.

"I didn't think you would be happy . . ." she mumbled. "But I meant what I said, Ian."

"I don't think ya did."

Abigail didn't want to argue anymore. She could stay and continue this verbal battle, but it was pointless. Even though denying her feelings for him had been a lie, she *had* meant what she said. Their relationship wasn't possible. And it wasn't worth pursuing.

At her response, he shook his head and turned to leave. But he reached for her hand just as she stepped onto a loose pile of gravel. Unable to steady herself, she slipped down the pond's edge, sending them both into the shallow pond.

She emerged from the cold water, shivering and a little miffed. Immediately she sloshed, dripping wet, toward the muddy shore, but he was too quick to let her make a break for it.

"Abby, wait," he said, and surprisingly she stopped.

She turned, pushing away pieces of wet hair from her face. "The night before you left," she whispered, "I watched you wash your wounds under the pump. I rushed outside . . . and was caught by the men who attacked you."

"What did they do to you?"

"They would've killed you—"

"*What* did they do to you?" he asked more firmly.

"Nothing," she said quickly. "They threatened that if I encouraged our relationship, they'd come after us both."

"They threatened me too."

"I figured. I came to you that morning just to make certain you were okay and to apologize. If I had told you this then, would you have stayed?"

With no hesitation, he answered, "Yes, I would have."

"Exactly. You had to leave while you still had time. After all that, I wasn't going to allow you to submit to any more torture because of me. They could have killed you, and I said what I thought was the right thing to do."

"You were protectin' me," he whispered. "Abby . . ." he breathed, reaching out to her.

She stared at his hand for a moment and then slowly placed her palm in his.

"Abby, everything I said to you that day . . . I didn't mean it."

She sniffed. "Yes, you did . . . and maybe I deserved it."

"If I knew then what I know now . . . I would've kept my distance, if only to keep ya safe. But I don't regret any minute spent in your company. You will always be beautiful to me. You will always be the kindest woman I know. And the bravest. I know the circumstances haven't changed, but I'd like to ask ya for one thing."

Abigail's sodden clothes made her shiver in the open air, but the warmth of Ian's hand was a welcoming contrast. She thought she'd be afraid or feel worried over what Ian would ask of her. Instead, she felt trust. And it was all she needed to hear him out.

"We never had the chance to finish what we started back in the stable that day."

Abigail's knees weakened a little. The butterflies in her stomach fluttered going back to the last tender moment they shared. And just as she did before, she felt anxious anticipation.

"No, we didn't," she said.

"'Tis a lot to ask of ya. But if I die tomorrow, I could do it without any regrets, knowing I had the chance to kiss Abigail Westmont."

Abigail could feel the ice in her heart crack. She hoped she knew what she was doing. But like Ian, she didn't want to live the rest of her life wondering either. She'd daydreamed of it for so long, and it was the kind of closure she wanted.

He waited patiently for her to give him an answer. And she did so by taking a step forward to meet him in the middle.

Carefully he leaned in to gently brush his lips against her cheek. His warmth washed over her like a heavy quilt on a winter night. She didn't expect his facial hair to feel soft, but with the way it brushed against her ear, she couldn't keep from giggling.

She hurried to bite her lip, hoping she didn't ruin the moment. But she felt Ian shaking in silent laughter, and they both met each other's eyes, smiling until his lips descended onto hers.

She'd thought of this moment many times since the day they met, but her imagination couldn't compare to how she felt now.

Ian pulled back slightly, exhaling a heavy breath that matched her sigh. But Abigail wasn't ready for it to end. It meant that what they shared was over and she wouldn't see him again. She'd be coaxed into marrying someone else, while a large piece of her heart remained with him.

To deny that she didn't love Ian would be like denying she needed air to breathe. It was almost better to leave well enough alone, to believe they were wrong for each other so she could move on.

His hands remained on her face. There was nothing more he could do or say to make her feel better. And before he could, she maneuvered herself from his warm embrace and hurried away.

"Abby," he called out, but she didn't dare look back.

She half expected him to chase after her but was grateful he didn't. She didn't want to leave that blissful moment at all, but a clean break was necessary. And she didn't want him to see the fresh tears streaming down her flushed face.

Abigail kept running until she reached a secluded part of the path, and she slumped down onto a large boulder. Out of breath, she rested her elbows on her knees and cried. She hadn't let herself feel sad for weeks, and of all things to blubber about, at least it had nothing to do with violent attackers or hateful words.

But as always, she stood tall and wiped away the moisture on her cheeks. She continued down the path in regal silence, hearing the chattering of two women around the bend. Abigail had no way to avoid Iris and Solana, who took one look at her and gasped.

"Abby, there you are," said Iris. "Why are your clothes soaked? Did you go for a swim?"

"You don't look well either," added Solana.

Abigail hurried for a response. "Yes."

"Yes to what?"

"Yes, I wasn't feeling well . . . so I went for a swim." Their eyes narrowed. "But I feel better now, and think I should change into dry clothes before I catch my death."

"A bath might help as well," said Iris, reaching out to pick a leaf out of her hair.

"Right, I'll leave you two to your walk."

"Actually," said Solana, "we came looking for you. There's been some development in the mystery of the masked man."

Abigail frowned. She hoped the faceless man wouldn't return. He reminded her too much of her masked attacker. "What about him?"

Iris scrunched up her nose. "First, let's get you cleaned up. News is better received when you don't smell like pond water."

Twenty-Two

As Phillip hammered in a new support beam for the Burnheart house, he saw Ian kick over a bucket of water, startling the horses grazing nearby. In a gesture of apology, Ian walked over to his own horse and began brushing her coat.

"What have I done?" Phillip heard Ian say, using a comforting voice. "For weeks I've thought nothin' but the worst of her. I go out to find me own way and get over it only to find myself right back where I started. Then I had to pull a stunt like that!"

The horse whinnied, and Ian smiled at her. "It doesn't change anythin'. Sayin' goodbye like that was obviously the wrong thing to do, and now I'm confused as ever."

Phillip decided to stop eavesdropping and make his presence known. "Talking to the horse again?" he called out.

Ian whirled around, his hand ready at the knife stowed in his saddlebag. He relaxed when he saw Phillip.

"One of these days you're going to get hurt because I couldn't control me own reflexes," said Ian.

Phillip simply chuckled. "I'd worry more about your horse turning on you. You never know when she'll start sharing your secrets with me."

Ian ignored the snide remark. "No, she'd never do that to me. Do ya need somethin'?"

"I could use some help with the floor."

Ian nodded and moved to the crate of tools to grab a hammer.

"You were back much later than you said you'd be," said Phillip. "And since you were trespassing on another man's land, I can only assume you're in a tight situation."

"How did you guess that?"

"There are two ponds in this whole area. One near Fairbrooke and another on the Rosenlund property. You rode in from the south, your clothes are soaking wet, and you're talking to your horse about leaving well enough alone."

"I don't want to talk about it."

"If it concerns Abigail, then I believe you should."

Ian's voice rose. "It's none of your business."

"Of course it's my business!" Phillip defended. "She would have been my sister-in-law. Now I say again, if it concerns Abigail, I'd like to know what happened."

Ian sighed. "We ran into each other. It wasn't planned, but we both said some things we've been holdin' in for a long while."

"And?" he coaxed.

"She hit me, we talked, we talked some more . . . and that's about it."

Phillip folded his arms disapprovingly, but quickly moved on. "Did you say why you were back?"

"No. I didn't tell her about you or Adam either."

Phillip nodded in relief. "Then what does this mean for you both?"

"It's over."

"Doesn't sound like you want it to be."

"Well, of course I don't want it to be over," Ian said, moving a loose floorboard into place. "But regardless of what *I* want, it is. And it ended on a positive note this time . . . mostly."

"Ian, why are you doing this to yourself? Unlike Adam and I, you aren't obligated to this land. You could rise in this world and become the man Abigail's father would approve of."

Ian shook his head as if to answer no, but said, "I don't know how."

"Well you need to figure it out soon. You're a good horse trainer, Ian. And a good breeder. Instead of working as a stable hand, go to Cedric and ask to become an apprentice. In time you'll learn the business and find success in that."

"The men who ran me off won't take kindly to that idea."

"You survived that and faced a band of smugglers in the same month. If all else fails, you start your own business. If I reclaim Fairbrooke, I'll invest in it."

"You're not sayin' that because I helped save your life, are ya?"

Phillip chuckled. "I can't promise you anything. But I saw potential in you long before I owed you my life. And Abigail saw your potential to make her happy. So don't let go of that idea just yet."

"You should probably take your own advice."

"I haven't with Iris."

"But you're making progress, aren't you?"

"I'm speaking to the solicitor this evening. He said he found something I'd needed to see. I can't be certain if it's progress or not, but it's more than what we've had in days."

"That's great news!" cried Ian. "This could be the game changer. And don't tell me not to get our hopes up. We need a bit of hope around here."

Phillip couldn't agree more. "I'll make you a deal," he said to Ian. "The day I show myself to Iris, you will tell Abigail how much you love her."

"Phillip," he warned.

"I mean it. It isn't as complicated as you're led to believe. You love the woman, and denying it is making you fall apart. And in front of your horse! So be a man and never let her go, before it's too late. You can make this right, just as I can."

Ian was lost in thought, and Phillip continued, "Think of it this way, at least we both have it better off than my brother."

Ian smiled and looked off into the distance. "Where did he run off to this time?"

"Where else? He's off to stop the impending betrothal of Solana Rosenlund and Camden Deveraux."

"Now there's a man with a death wish."

The two of them finished the flooring, and Phillip could now appreciate the Burnheart manor a bit more now that all the rotted wood had been replaced.

The house was turning into a substantial home, and if Phillip reclaimed Fairbrooke like he planned to, Adam could very well live there too—and he could lease Burnheart to Ian if he chose to. Ian could start his business as a horse breeder, and his future could flourish there.

Though thinking of such things would be getting his hopes up, they needed more hope in their lives, and he let himself feel hopeful on his long ride to London.

Phillip arrived at the old tavern wearing Ian's borrowed clothes and cap. He made a note to use Adam's renovation fund to purchase new ones for Ian. Though Ian generally kept himself clean, he switched back and forth between two sets, and he deserved something nicer to represent himself.

Phillip entered the establishment, scanning the room of loud patrons until he spotted the short, balding man in the corner. He approached his table, and without asking, took his seat across from him.

"Mr. Harris," Phillip acknowledged.

"Sir," he replied, shaking his hand. "Thank you for agreeing to meet with me in this less-than-formal setting."

"I've been in worse."

"Right. Let's get on with it then. I looked into Richard's receipts like you asked. There have been some withdrawals from the company accounts, and so far he's claiming its use for rebuilding Fairbrooke. But look here," he said, sliding a piece of paper in front of Phillip to look at.

Phillip glanced at the written total and scowled. "There's nothing money could do to rebuild that land unless he hired extra workers to replant the orchard. But I saw the land for myself, and nothing has changed."

"Exactly. And there was a large deposit put into a personal account the week of your disappearance—but not Richard's account. Camden's."

"Is telling me that legal?"

"It's the reason I'm telling you here and not in the office."

"Fair enough. This is groundbreaking, but I don't think it's enough to prove him guilty."

"But there's something more. Look there," he said, gesturing to the top of the page. "Richard has been sending money annually to a small town near Yorkshire. He claims it to be his sister, but he didn't start until this date right here."

Phillip did the math but didn't see the significance. "Twenty-seven years. Should that mean something?"

"Camden is twenty-seven years old."

Phillip's eyes widened. "Are you suggesting that Richard has been sending money to his birth mother?"

"Any man would want to keep quiet about his son's illegitimacy. It's a stretch, but either way, if Richard has been sending money and was running out, he was taking from the company funds to do it."

"And you didn't catch this until now?" When Mr. Harris didn't answer, Phillip understood. "He paid you to overlook it."

Mr. Harris cleared his throat. "He threatened me, actually. And it was a threat I couldn't ignore. But the second you showed up on my doorstep, I learned the extent of what Richard is capable of, and I'm hoping you will overlook this indiscretion if I make things right."

"We all make mistakes under pressure," said Phillip. "But you must testify in court, if Richard is going to be brought to justice."

"Absolutely."

"Thank you, Mr. Harris. Not just for your honesty, but for truly restoring what I'd almost given up. Hope."

Twenty-Three

Solana stared down at her plate, knowing if she looked up, Camden would still be staring at her in that way she had grown to hate.

She attempted to listen to the conversation their fathers were discussing, but the sound of her heartbeat in her ears drowned everything out.

"Do you agree, Solana?" she heard someone say.

She looked up, unsure of who was addressing her. "Sorry?"

Camden chuckled. "The coast would make an excellent retreat for one to spend a few weeks this time of year, don't you think?"

"Um . . . I guess so. I've never been," she answered.

Right away Solana knew that was the wrong thing to say. Camden's eyes lit up as he said, "A good friend of mine recommended it after spending his honeymoon there. Said I was welcome to use his summer cottage whenever I liked."

The food in her stomach churned suddenly. "Well, isn't that generous. Papa," she said abruptly, changing the subject, "I heard you helped Mr. Davies today. How did that go?"

He shrugged. "Just fine, dear. Helped him repair his wagon, which took a great deal of time, but I'm glad the work is done and now in the presence of close friends and family," he said, raising his glass. Margaret did the same as she patted Solana's knee under the table.

At this point she knew it was best to simply keep her mouth shut. Any word she spoke would only increase their anticipation of what was yet to come, and she wasn't ready for it yet. She had no time to prepare to disappoint them, and she feared that if she declined, she'd end up without a choice in the end.

The image of Camden holding her hand on their wedding day came to mind. But she was quick to replace his face and touch with another's. Though it was a faded memory, Solana remembered the specific moment Adam Garrow had held her in his arms. They were dire circumstances, but the mere thought of his gentle touch caused her to feel more than anything she had ever felt.

It was silly to believe that it could ever happen, seeing as he had failed to show since the night of the party. But at least it helped her become aware of the better life she knew she deserved.

Once everyone finished, they all proceeded into the drawing room, and Solana caught Faye's arm, stopping them in the middle of the hall.

"Go ahead," Solana said when Camden stopped to wait for them. "I only wish to speak with my sister in private for a moment."

She didn't miss the crease in his brow that quickly changed to a courteous smile as he said, "Of course," and eventually followed their families out of sight.

"Faye, I think I'm going to faint," she breathed, letting fade the pleasant disposition she had been feigning all evening.

"Really?"

"Yes! I cannot do this, and you must tell me I can. I don't know what else to do."

Faye then took her shoulders and looked deeply into her eyes. "I know you can do this, sister. You are the strongest person I know. Camden is a good man who will love you and take care of you. But . . . if he doesn't make you happy—and I know he doesn't— then you shouldn't marry him. It will only kill your spirit."

Solana was shocked. Never had she heard such words of wisdom come from her young sister's mouth. "Faye—?"

She shook her head. "I may be young, but I know more than you think."

"What if they force my fate into Camden's hands anyway?"

"Run away." Faye shrugged. "I'll marry him, and you can live your life the way you've always dreamed of."

"Over my dead body," Solana retorted, appalled with the idea of her young sister married to anyone such as Camden. She didn't know why the thought provoked that reaction, but the image chilled her.

Faye chuckled. "I only jest . . . somewhat. Solana, our parents are not fools, and they love us more than anything. They only want what is best. Talk to them first."

"I wish it were that simple."

"How is it not?"

Solana shook her head and embraced Faye affectionately. "Promise me you will never grow older. Just stay this young forever."

"If that ever happened, I would hope a higher power would strike me down immediately."

Solana smiled and took in a labored breath. "We should go before we're missed."

"If you like, I can say you have taken ill."

"No. Tell them I went out for some cool night air on the veranda. And I'll be there in a short minute."

"Will that only provoke Camden to seek you out for some time . . . alone?" Faye asked.

"Exactly. I need speak to him alone. You're right: if I am to end this, it must be now and in the least painful way possible. I can only hope he has enough compassion to understand."

"Me too."

Solana watched Faye disappear around the corner before making her way to the terrace that overlooked the orchard. The sun had just set, casting hard shadows on the greenery below, silhouetted with orange light that slowly began to fade on the horizon.

Her father spent most of his leisure time there. Above it was an overhanging garden where vines wove through the wooden beams that crossed each other. Every small opening was filled with roses of varying bright colors.

"I believe Shakespeare wrote a scene such as this," she heard a voice say, and she turned to see Camden sauntering through the double doors. "Needed some fresh air?"

"Just a bit," she said, suddenly losing her nerve. "Shall we?"

"Actually, I hoped to have a moment with you alone," he said, leaning against the rail so he could study her. "Tell me, do you believe our relationship has grown since we've known each other?"

"Um, yes, I believe we have become well acquainted," she answered.

"*Just* well acquainted?"

Solana swallowed hard and sighed. "Instead of this usual back and forth, will you please tell me what it is you wish for?"

His eyes widened at her blunt tone. "I only wish to please you. I wish you wouldn't seem so frightened of me."

"I'm sorry; it's not my intention to appear so."

He chuckled at her response. "Ah, so you do fear me, but you only wish to put on a mask for the people around you."

"No . . . I just—"

"I only jest," he interrupted. "I don't wish to beat around the bush, so I won't delay in saying that I have grown fond of you over these past months. And I know as time goes on that fondness will eventually grow into something far greater than that. Which is why, knowing the good woman you were raised to be," he said, placing his hand over hers, "you have boundless potential to make a superior wife."

Solana smirked at his choice of words, but he didn't seem to notice. She could tell he was trying to be sincere, but she wasn't sure if he was even complimenting her.

"And I believe I could make a superior husband to you, Miss Rosenlund."

There it was—the proposal. It was most certainly not how she dreamed it would be. She imagined something a little more heart-felt and some sort of confession of love. His eyes had no evidence of a man in love at all. Judging by his spoken words, a good wife seemed to be the only thing he was searching for, along with the perks that came with the marriage document.

"Mr. Deveraux, I do wish you would tell me what it is you're so fond of."

"You do not see it yourself?"

"I just want to hear you say it," she said, slightly hoping to hear what she longed for a man to say to woo a woman. But coming from Camden, she figured it wouldn't mean very much.

He mulled it over for a second. "And what is it that you want me to say?"

"You're missing the point. I don't wish to put words into your mouth. I wish to know why you want me to be your wife."

He hesitated once more. "Because I have strong feelings for you that I cannot deny."

"By the *way* you say it, I find that very hard to believe. Do I not have any other qualities besides how I was raised? What are these feelings you speak of? Are they feelings of love, adoration . . . ?"

"Miss Rosenlund, look at your parents. Do you see the love they have for each other?"

"Of course I do."

He sighed in what seemed like mild irritation. "People in our position don't usually start out that way. Women are married off to men for the sake of retaining the ironclad chain that is their fam-ily's welfare. Now I know for certain that your father and mother's engagement was arranged and short lived, but they started off as friends, and that fondness grew. I look at you and see that if you don't marry soon, some scruffy, weathered old man will ask for your hand, and your parents will have no choice but to tie you to him because you refused to meet your duty when you had the chance. I know your father. He will see you married off whether you like it or not."

"How dare you make such an insinuation?"

"I only speak the truth. You may not like it, but it had to be said. I am offering you a chance at happiness. As you can see, I am young and well fit enough to care for you, which I already do. And if you can just picture our life together, you will see that it is far better than any other option you have. You will live near your home and raise our children in the same surroundings you grew up in. All I ask is that you think about it."

Solana opened her mouth to speak, but no words came. She wasn't expecting such an explanation.

The way Camden spoke, it sounded like he was trying to convince her of a business deal—one that she couldn't deny was hard to turn down. If she had to pick her lowest moment, it was this one.

He touched her hand once more, but she barely felt it. She could think of a far better option, but it would mean giving up her home and leaving a heavy burden on her family, a point Camden was clearly trying to make.

"I hate to see anything bad happen to you, or your sister for that matter," he said, feigning concern, but to her it sounded almost malicious. "I can see this is a lot for you take in. I say again, think on it, and let us return to our families for the time being. I'm sure they are curious as to what is taking us so long."

He offered his arm to her, and she reluctantly took it. He was acting completely out of character.

He led her to where their families sat and conversed about trivial things. The second they entered, everyone fell silent and directed their attention toward her. Camden gestured something to his father, and his shoulders slumped, likely accepting the message that she didn't give an answer to his question. Christopher noticed it as well, and Margaret seemed to be the only one to break the silent tension Solana brought in.

"Hello darling, you don't look well. Is everything all right?"

Solana put on her false smile and said, "Yes, everything is . . . fine."

Everything was most certainly *not* fine, but she played her part well. About thirty minutes into a game of whist, Arietta arrived with a sealed note in her hand.

"Miss Rosenlund, this was left on the doorstep for you."

All eyes were on her as Solana stood to accept the folded piece of parchment.

"Well read it, dear," her mother said. "Who is it from?"

Solana was hesitant to find out in front all the onlookers, but figured she'd look suspicious if she chose not to. She proceeded to break the seal.

Solana,

I haven't forgotten my promise. If you choose to meet me there, I will be at the town livery tomorrow morning at nine o'clock. I know it's a long way to travel, but it's public, and I fear if I ask to meet in the orchard, you'd believe my intentions improper. I assure you my only wish is to talk and answer your questions.

~ The masked party-crasher

"Well?" asked Camden, as though he had the right to know her business.

"Oh, it's . . . it's a thank you note from Mrs. Townsend," she lied. "For the gift I sent her new baby."

She *had* sent Mrs. Townsend a gift for her baby, and everyone seemed to buy the lie as they returned to their activities.

Back at the game table, Solana tucked the note into her sleeve and tried the rest of the night to stay focused. Thinking about the note, she decided that before she rode into town, she'd try one more time asking her parents what they weren't telling her.

When the Deverauxs had finally left, Solana was about to follow Faye up the stairs before she stopped to face her parents in the parlor.

Her mother spoke first. "My dear, is there something you wish to tell us?"

"Actually . . . there is something I wish for *you* to tell me." Her mother's brow puckered, but Solana maintained a calm expression. "I want you both to tell me about the fire."

Solana waited patiently for her answer, and finally her father broke the silence this time. "Dear, we already told you all we know."

"I don't believe you did," she said boldly. "I deserved to know all the details. Whatever you both are protecting me from, I can handle it."

Her mother sighed as her father sat down on the settee. He closed his eyes and pinched the bridge of his nose. "When I saw the wildfire break out on the Garrows' land, I rushed over to see if I could help, but the flames were too great. There was nothing that could be done but to evacuate the tenants and get everyone to safety. I arrived in time to see Caleb's son carrying you to me. You were barely conscious."

Solana nodded. "I remember being in the orchard before waking up in the smoke."

"I took you home, where a physician came shortly after. You were asleep for a long time. He noticed the bruise on your head and said you may have suffered a concussion and most likely wouldn't wake up if that were the case."

Solana became thoughtful. "How did Phillip know I was there?"

"We assumed he was at the right place at the right time."

"So neither of you saw Adam Garrow with him." Solana watched her parents exchanged worrisome looks. "

Her father stood. "How do you know about Adam Garrow?"

"He was there that day, and from your reactions, I think you two know that already. Why did you want to keep his presence a secret?"

Her mother sighed, standing to be near her father's side. "He isn't to be trusted."

"Why not?" she asked, and she was about to bring up his role in saving her, but her mother continued to speak.

"We were going to tell you about the merger years ago. When you were young, we discussed the idea you and Adam Garrow marrying."

At that moment, Solana's world completely altered. "We were betrothed?"

"Yes, but after he left his home years ago, we broke it off immediately," her father said. "Everything was falling apart for them, and we didn't want you dragged into all of it. And we surely didn't want a suspect of arson ever getting near you."

Solana took a moment absorb that information. "Is that why you are pushing me to marry Camden? To merge our lands together to build your empire?"

"There is no need to talk that way," her mother scolded.

She ignored her reprimand. "What if I refuse to marry him?"

"You will not refuse," Christopher said firmly. "I'm sorry, Solana. I know you've always been a free spirit, but as your father, it's time that I see that your future security is set. End of discussion."

He left the room without another word. Solana's mother reached out for her hands, and Solana expected to hear words of comfort, but instead her mother said, "Your father is right. One day you will understand."

Solana was heartbroken. In just a few short minutes, her entire world had turned upside down, and *still* she was left with the same questions—if not more. After retiring to her room, she took the note from her dress sleeve and made a decision.

Tomorrow she would see him again. She'd have her questions answered, and above all, she'd learn more about the man behind the mask.

TWENTY-FOUR

Solana made it to the town livery at five minutes to nine. Though before she could walk her horse to the stall, the man she knew to be Adam Garrow was already there waiting for her.

Solana let out a ragged breath, willing her nerves to calm down. In one hand, he held a half-eaten apple, and wore a black glove on the other. They locked eyes just as he gave her a crooked smile. "You made it," he said.

"You said something about providing answers to my questions, and I am eager to hear them."

"Would you prefer to stay here or walk a bit?"

"I don't mind walking."

He stepped forward, offering to take the reins, and she passed them over. But before leading her horse to the stall, he offered the apple to the horse, and Solana had a bout of déjà vu. From her memories of him in the orchard, she recalled more about when they first met. It still felt like a dream, but mixed around in a different order.

Together they walked the path near the shops, and he broke the silence by saying, "You asked me who I was . . ."

"And in the recent days, I've remembered who you are," she said.

His eyes narrowed. "You do?"

"An injured mind has a way of repressing even the most memorable parts of our lives. But here is what I *do* know. Your name is Adam Garrow. We met in the orchard the day before the fire, the same fire you saved me from. You kissed me . . . twice, I believe. And . . . you and I were once intended to marry."

Adam's heart fell. He wasn't prepared for this yet. He had planned to tell her when the time was right, when he could explain himself fully and with utmost sincerity. But her family had beaten him to it.

"Did you know?" she asked. She was completely expressionless, but he promised her answers.

"Yes . . . I did," he answered honestly.

"Was it a game to you, then? When we first met that day, was flirting with me a means of amusement for you?"

"Of course not," he defended, disappointed but not surprised that she would jump to that conclusion.

"Please tell me then, why are you here?" she pled, her eyes looking more brilliant as fresh tears threatened to spill over.

"I was young when I found out about the merger. I had no real idea who you were. Our parents were good friends, but they felt it better for us to grow up a bit before bringing us together. But when I discovered who I really was—"

"I know. You left for a few years to find yourself."

"I left to find the headstone of my birth father," he corrected.

Her eyes softened. "Oh."

"When I found the grave of my birth father, I had the closure I needed, and I came home. And when I made it onto the property, I saw you. I didn't recognize you at first. When I did, I attempted to leave and go about my business. But you were so kind and encouraging. And I really did need a bath."

That earned him a smile from her, which reassured him to continue. "I was told I act impulsively sometimes. And I agree. I wanted to get to know you, and that's why I asked to see you again."

"That's why I was in the orchard."

He nodded. "The next morning I was with my family. We made our amends, but then we all saw the flames. I ran into it knowing you'd be there."

Adam reached for his glove on his scarred hand, removing it to show the evidence, then unbuttoned his sleeve and pushed up the fabric. He heard her breath catch, and she stepped forward to take a closer look.

"Good heavens," she said, sympathy in her tone.

"When I found you, you had blood on your face. You weren't breathing, so I carried you out of the smoke—"

"And you put air back into my lungs again," she finished. "I heard Phillip right after."

"He took you to your father and then assisted with my wounds. I was later sent to a place to convalesce," he said, rolling down his sleeve. "After that, I regained full strength in my arm and most of the use in my fingers."

"You suffered this because of me."

"*You* suffered this because of me. You wouldn't have been in the orchard if not—"

"I hit my head. That wasn't your fault. That could have happened to me on any other given day, and no one would have known for hours."

"Well, that's generous of you to look at it that way. Do you remember how you hit your head?"

"It's so foggy, it's even hard to remember what I had for breakfast that morning. It's speculated that I fell out of tree, which seems to make sense. But on one hand, it feels like there's more."

"I can understand that."

Solana tilted her head toward the path, gesturing for him to continue their walk. "You were at your mother's funeral."

"By then I was told about your memory. I hoped seeing me would have sparked something, but at the time I was being investigated for arson, which I'm sure you know about."

"Don't you have an alibi? You were with your family at the time."

"It wasn't strong enough, so I decided to keep myself busy by rebuilding the home my father left me. By then Phillip had fallen in love, and he became engaged to Iris Westmont."

"Is he still alive?" she asked abruptly, and Adam looked at her. He wasn't planning on saying anything more about him, but her question threw him off.

"Why do you ask?"

"Iris refuses to believe he is dead. I know it's a long shot, but if you do know anything, I must give her peace of mind."

Adam had to think quickly. He didn't want to share an important secret, but Phillip was the major reason why he was there. He wanted to trust her, but given how close she was to the Westmont family, he struggled to answer. "I received word of his disappearance and used one of his ships to go looking for him. Eventually, I *did* find him. He's alive, but he's just not here."

"What?" she exclaimed. "Where is he? Is he safe?"

"He's safe," he assured. "Just recovering, much like I had to."

"Oh my goodness," she sighed. "Iris will be thrilled."

Adam lightly touched her shoulder to stop her. "You mustn't say anything to her."

"Why not?"

"Phillip is fighting a battle right now. There's someone out there who wants him dead, and if Iris knows, she's put at risk. I wish I could say more, but it's no longer my place."

Solana lowered her head into her hands, rubbing at her eyes. "That is a hard secret to keep."

"One you won't have to keep for long. But I trust that you will." Impulsively, he took her hands and held them in a way meant to be comforting. "I'm sorry for all the stress you have encountered."

Adam felt her squeeze his hands, accepting his gesture. Then she asked, "Why me? I know why you stayed with me that afternoon in the orchard. But after you came back, why did you dance with me like that at the party?"

That question he could easily answer. "I knew there was a chance your father would never let me near you if I said who I was. I just wanted one opportunity to be close to you again before that chance was out the window for good. And besides, you looked very miserable with poor Camden Deveraux."

She laughed at that, and he appreciated the sound just as much as when he heard it the first time.

"Solana . . . if I ever had a fighting chance with you, would you have accepted my request to court you formally?"

Her brow furrowed as she gave him a once over. "Maybe."

"I promise to never address you as Blossom."

That made her laugh harder. "Oh goodness, it's coming back to me."

Slowly and deliberately, he brought her hands up to his lips and let go. Now that they were in a good place with each other, it was the boldest he dared to be until all was said and done.

"I'm glad right now we can at least be friends," Adam said. He didn't want their interlude to end, but he walked her back to the livery, lest she'd be missed.

"I assume I'll see you again?" she asked as they reached the stall.

"Hopefully. As you noticed at the party, I do like to make a big show of things. Next time, however, I'll ask before I steal you off the dance floor."

She chuckled. "I'll be watching for you, then."

"And I will find the next possible opportunity."

"Soon, I hope," she said, mounting her horse. With the click of her tongue, her horse trotted down the street.

With a heavy sigh, he said out loud, "I hope so too."

Twenty-Five

───── ⚬ ─────

Solana stood in front of the full-length mirror wearing the most beautiful dress she'd ever seen. The fabric was a lovely shade of blue and the neckline was squarely cut. It was the most elegant she'd ever felt, and she was grateful her parents spared no expense in making her feel like a proper lady. Her mother stood on one side of her and Arietta on the other as they fussed over every detail.

"This will be the most prestigious event of the season," said her mother.

They were always prestigious, but in this case, she was right. Lord Chamberlin threw himself the grandest birthday party every year, and though many were invited, few who lived outside of London were fortunate enough to be a guest. Solana had a feeling that Mr. Deveraux had a hand in getting them on the list.

Solana entertained the idea of Adam showing up, mask and all. The chances were slim, but she wouldn't mind having another dance with him. In fact, when he asked her if he stood a chance, she'd wanted to say yes. She wanted another opportunity to get to know him under better circumstances. Hopefully they would, but until then she would attend this ball and wait for everything to play out naturally.

"Come now!" Arietta exclaimed. "The carriage has arrived!"

On cue, Solana met Abigail and Iris in the front room, looking exquisite in their gowns—Iris in a rose color, with matching flowers in her hair, and Abigail in green with embroidered silk gloves.

They finally arrived at sundown, fashionably late, and the second she stepped through the front gate, Solana understood the meaning of prestigious. The hall, the tables, the courtyard, and the people . . . all were lavishly decorated, as if the artistic architecture itself weren't enough to impress.

The atmosphere held an air of royalty, causing anyone with Solana's upbringing to feel immensely humble. What amazed her most was the Gothic look it maintained. She felt like she'd fallen into a tale of King Arthur's time.

Unfortunately, she was reminded of the current reality when her mother practically dragged her across the room as soon as she spotted Mr. Deveraux and Camden amongst the crowd.

"Mrs. Rosenlund, what a pleasure it is," said Mr. Deveraux, bowing in respect.

Her mother gave a slight curtsy, and Solana mimicked the same gesture to Camden, feeling his thorough gaze upon her. Without breaking eye contact, he took her hand and kissed it, causing her arm to feel cold as ice. Not at all what she felt when Adam had kissed her hands.

"A pleasure indeed," said Camden. "Will you accompany me for the next dance?"

Knowing she couldn't deny him, she gave a brief nod. Her mother cleared her throat.

"I would be delighted," Solana corrected, holding back the scowl she wanted to throw at her mother for her persistence.

Camden beamed, holding out his arm. She reluctantly took it and followed him to the dance floor. Being more familiar with folk dances than formal ones, Solana felt inadequate, especially being in a room with onlookers who ranked in nobility.

"You look stunning," he said, taking his position.

"Thank you," she managed to say before the music began.

During the dance, Camden attempted conversation with her, but the lively tune and large crowd prevented it. In any other circumstance, Solana would've enjoyed the dance. She was fond of the court dances. But as soon as it ended, Camden nearly dragged her off toward the mingling crowd while swallowing a full glass of wine from the food tables.

Solana tried to appear indifferent, but because it was out of character for him to look so disheveled, even for a moment, keeping herself in his company felt like a chore as usual. She didn't care much for men who favored strong drinks.

"Miss R-Rosenlund . . ." he stammered. "I believe there is a conversation we still need to continue."

As prepared as she thought she was for this moment, Solana's breath shook as she became fully aware of the large crowd listening closely.

"I do not believe this is the time or place."

"And when will it ever be the time or place?" he snapped.

His eyes blazed briefly, and she was tempted to step back, but she dared not show any weakness. Fortunately, his previous demeanor returned and he spoke softer. "I was hoping to announce our . . . our engagement this evening. But I cannot until you have given me your answer."

No! I will not marry you!

"I . . ." she squeaked, her words catching in her throat. Suddenly the crowd became a bit too quiet.

Camden's attention was abruptly averted. Over the music that still played, she heard him curse under his breath. Once the silence turned into garbled murmurs, she pulled herself away to better view what everyone was gawking at.

And then she saw him. Walking with a confident stride, clean shaven, wearing formal attire, and with both hands in black leather gloves.

Adam!

His name nearly sounded from her lips, and she swallowed hard. Ignoring everyone's curious glances, Adam happily turned about the room and approached the host. They shook hands and greeted each other welcomingly, which signaled for everyone to relax and go about their business.

Solana could hardly breathe. And by the way Camden appeared to be fuming, he was *not* pleased with the surprise arrival. She had a feeling this night would become far more interesting than she'd planned.

Solana felt utterly ridiculous as Camden took hold of her wrist and began dragging her to who knows where.

"Where are you taking me?" she asked, aghast at his abrasive move. When he didn't respond, panic grew within her and she dug her heels, tugging her wrist more forcefully. "Camden, stop!"

He froze in his tracks, and Solana stumbled into him before regaining her composure.

"What on earth is going on?" she asked, finally pulling her wrist free.

Camden didn't answer. He was distracted once again as his eyes darted over her head. Solana turned and saw Adam walking—no, strutting—toward them with a look that quickly changed from stern to . . . mischievous.

She immediately felt her face grow warm, and she couldn't suppress the smile etched across her lips. She had to keep her wits about her though. Although she knew him, she remembered that she wasn't supposed to, and she had to play the part.

"Who is that?" she asked, feigning ignorance.

"No one you need to concern yourself with," said Camden, reaching for her wrist once more, but Solana dodged him quite gracefully. "Solana, please. We must leave."

"You, sir, are not my father," she retaliated.

"Do not be stubborn. Now come."

"Camden," she heard Adam say, and she turned around to see him approach, giving Camden a curt nod.

"Adam," he grumbled.

"It's been a long time. How do you fair these days?"

"Quite well."

"Bet you do."

The following silence as they stared each other down left Solana ill at ease, and she wondered what to say in this situation. Solana could imagine Adam's knuckles turning white from the fist he was holding so tightly. They obviously knew each other in the past. But what could have happened to trigger this instant tension between them?

"Excuse me," Solana interjected, and both eyes were on her. "Would you be so kind as to introduce me to your friend?"

She could tell Camden was subconsciously fighting with himself at the moment. And seeing him squirm after his moment of austerity was a private victory to her.

"Camden is not one to give introductions," said Adam. "He doesn't feel like it's his place to do so. Besides, I know very well how to say my own name, and I already know who you are, Miss Rosenlund. A true pleasure it is to formally reacquaint myself with you."

In another place and time, this was probably how they would have met. Yet, oddly, she preferred the orchard much more.

She curtsied, dipping her head. "The pleasure is mine. And what do I address you as?"

"Adam," he said casually, releasing her hand.

"And what is your surname?"

He smiled at her knowingly. "Just Adam. I'm not partial to people acknowledging me by my surname. Or my title for that matter."

"That's because he has none," Camden scoffed.

"I believe one's Christian name makes the person, not one's title," he defended. "Why, this lovely woman here is a perfect example of that. *Solana Rosenlund,*" he emphasized. "She lives up to her name completely. A ray of sun that shines on a delicate rose."

"Thank you. I appreciate the poetic inflection."

Camden rolled his eyes. "Any man can memorize a poetic verse. It is his character that should be admired."

"My greatest wish is to be a man worth admiring," Adam said. "Though I have my faults, would you, Miss Rosenlund, be willing to put that aside and make my one night's wish come true this evening by joining me in the next dance?"

"Actually—" Camden began to protest, but Solana cut him off before he could finish.

"It would be my pleasure."

Adam offered her his arm, and she took it gladly. He led her to the dance floor, leaving Camden fuming behind them.

Standing in position, he looked down at her, and Solana couldn't keep her delight down any longer.

She chuckled. "You do like to make a show of things."

"Surprised?" he said as they began the dance.

"Hardly," she said, keeping her voice low. "Crashing parties *is* your forte."

"Actually, I was invited this time."

"Really?"

He shrugged. "James Chamberlin was a friend of my father."

"Well, it's good to see you not risking your neck for once."

"*I'm* not risking much, but I did bring a few guests who are risking quite a bit this evening."

"Who?"

"You'll find out soon enough."

Their conversation paused for the rest of the dance, and her curiosity was more piqued than ever. But at the end, he bowed like a gentleman and quickly disappeared into the crowd.

It was pointless to chase after him. Whatever mission he was on now, she simply had to wait for it happen. But as soon as Solana made it to the sidelines, Iris found her.

"That man you were just dancing with. It was him, wasn't it?"

"Um," Solana said, knowing she wasn't supposed to say anything, especially to Iris, but she had her cornered. "What?"

"Don't play daft. He may have been in a mask, but I recognize his other features. Did you ask him? Does he know anything about Phillip?"

"We were dancing, Iris," she sighed. "It wasn't the right place to ask."

Iris groaned. "I must find him. Did he say where he went?"

"No, but—"

Iris turned on her heel and left with a determined look in her eye. Solana hoped that Abigail was at least having a better night than her sister.

Lantern in hand, Ian walked through the stables and admired the horses James Chamberlin had maintained over the years. Just by looking he could tell they were very well bred and cared for by a good stableman. He wondered if Mr. Chamberlin would have any need to hire another, but he greatly doubted it, although he was certain Adam could pull a few strings.

He'd specifically requested Ian to be at the largest fountain by eight-thirty. He wasn't too sure why, but he had a feeling it had something to do with Abigail Westmont. He only agreed to come as support for Adam, but feeling smart in his new clothes, he was curious to see how Abigail would react.

But once he made it to the fountain, he sat there alone for twenty minutes until Adam arrived. "What are you doing here alone?" he asked.

"That's what I'm wonderin'," Ian said. "Been alone this whole time. Was Abigail supposed to show?"

"Yes, I left her a note saying it was from you."

Ian wanted to smack him upside the head. "That was your first mistake!"

"I watched her read it, and she smiled."

"Most smiles on women aren't real, Adam. That's the first rule a man learns."

"Ian, quiet. I watched her head to the fountain myself."

"Then she changed her mind last minute. Adam, I appreciate ya wantin' to help, but I'm doin' this me own way. That's final. Now if I were you, I'd fetch Phillip from the guest room. Isn't his grand entrance supposed to be made soon?" he asked, pushing past Adam.

Heading into the manor, Ian found his way into an empty corridor for some solitude. He wandered far enough to not hear the music anymore, and he leaned against a wooden door, closing his eyes for a bit of peace.

He managed a few minutes before he heard the sound of footsteps to his left. But by the time he looked over, an explosion of pain went off in his skull.

It took a few disoriented seconds to realize he'd been struck in the head by something. Ian flipped over, fearing history repeating itself. But this time he didn't hesitate. He kicked at the figure looming over him.

The figure stumbled backward, enough for Ian to jump to his feet. In this dim lamplight, he couldn't recognize his attacker, but they were unevenly matched when the figure pulled out a knife.

"You can't have her!" the attacker screamed, lunging forward.

Ian twisted out of the way, grabbing the man's arm and elbowing him in the stomach. He then took his wrist and forced him to drop the knife to the floor. But as Ian hurried to grab it, the attacker kicked Ian's side, and the knife skid across stone.

They both went for the knife, and Ian looked up in time to see a vase crash over the scrawny man's head. He dropped to the floor, and behind him stood a woman wearing a green dress. Ian didn't have to stare long to know that it was Abigail who stood there, hands shaking and eyes wide with shock over what she just did.

When the scrawny man groaned, Ian tugged at his cravat, pulling it away to tie up the unconscious man's wrists.

Though his head throbbed, he couldn't help but laugh. "How in the world are ya here?" he asked Abigail.

"I . . . I . . ." she stammered, taking in heavy breaths. "I was headed to the fountain when I saw you entering the corridor. Bromley was right behind you, and I got suspicious he was up to no good."

"Ya know this man?"

"He was your replacement after you left. He drove us here."

"Well that figures," he said, doubling the knot. Sure that it was tight, he stood to open a door to a random room and dragged Bromley inside.

"Will you do me a favor?" he asked her, feeling his world start to spin. "Fetch Adam Garrow for me . . . because I'm about to pass out."

Abigail watched as Ian fell to the ground unconscious. This was not good, not good at all. After a bout of victory taking down the man who she suspected to be her stalker, she panicked.

She didn't want to leave him there, but trying to rouse him awake did nothing, and there was nothing else she could besides hurry back into the grand ballroom to look for the man Phillip asked for. She had no idea who Adam Garrow was, but he had the same surname as Phillip. Could they be related somehow? Why did Ian want his help?

Frantically, Abigail made her way through the ballroom, asking every guest she passed if they knew of an Adam Garrow, but none knew where he went. When she felt a tap on her shoulder, she turned to see James Chamberlin, the host himself.

"Did you say you were looking for Adam Garrow?"

"Yes. Do you know where he is? It's an emergency."

"Of course, right this way," he said, taking her across the entire ballroom, up the staircase, and into a separate wing, where he knocked on the door. "What is your name?" he asked her.

"Abigail Westmont."

"There is an Abigail Westmont here to see you," he said through the door.

The door opened to reveal a man she'd seen before. He was the one who gave her the letter about Phillip's disappearance.

"Miss Westmont, what are you doing here?" he asked.

"It's Ian. He's injured and asking for you."

"What happened to him?"

Abigail didn't want to become emotional, but she couldn't stop herself when the words began to spill out. "He's been hit over the head by a horrible man who wouldn't leave me alone. I knocked him out first, but I don't know what to do. Ian's unconscious—"

Adam shushed her, stepping out into the corridor. But when he did so, another man appeared behind him, and Abigail gasped. *Phillip!*

"Abigail, I know it's a shock to see me," Phillip said, which was the understatement of the year. "But we both would like to know where he is."

"South corridor," she choked.

"Best we take the long way," said Adam. "And Abigail, walk with us. You look a bit faint."

Abigail quietly followed them down a spiral staircase that led into a large library and connected with the east wing. Through a maze of connecting rooms, they entered the south corridor to find Ian no longer unconscious, but holding a wooden door closed with all his strength.

Phillip strode faster. "She said you were unconscious."

"I was, and so was he," he grunted as the door rattled from fists pounding behind it.

"Are you all right?" Phillip asked.

"I'm fine. Just had a dizzy spell."

"Let go," said Adam. "It's three against one now. I'm sure he'll calm down once he sees that."

Ian released his grip on the handle, and the door flung open. Abigail watched in awe as the three stood side by side, tall and steadfast, like brothers in arms. Bromley froze on the spot and fell to his knees.

TWENTY-SIX

———— ·⁙· ————

Phillip stood in the center, watching Bromley's stunned reaction as he whispered, "No. You're supposed to be dead."

"Sorry to disappoint," said Phillip, "but I'm very much alive, and Mr. Chamberlin will gladly make sure you're in shackles before the night is through."

Bromley began to chuckle to himself, his laughter growing louder and louder until he was in a fit of hysteria.

"This is a dream. You can't be alive," Bromley said, his eyes dancing with humor one moment and flooding with pure anger the next. "Deveraux paid me to do it. Tip off the smugglers, and in return, he'd help me take that no-good Irishman's place."

Phillip felt as though he'd been punched in the stomach. Without knowing it, they'd all shared the same enemy, and the catalyst was staring him right in the face.

"Abigail," said Bromley. He scrambled to lean forward to better look at her, but Adam held him back. "Everything I did was for you. It's *me* you should love, *me* who gave you the hair piece, *me* who watched you—"

Without thinking twice, Phillip grabbed the back of Bromley's shirt and pulled him to his feet.

"Phillip!" Ian shouted.

"Don't worry," he said. "I personally want to see to it that he rots away in a prison, just as he intended for me. Take care of Abigail, Ian. And Adam, tell Christopher Rosenlund to meet us by the carriages."

Abigail was about ready to slump to the floor when Ian caught her and pulled her into his arms. She held onto him tightly, feeling his cheek rest against her hair.

"Thank you," she mumbled, a fresh tear spilling down her cheek.

"It wasn't me who hit him over the head," he said.

"I meant for coming back. I kept giving you so many reasons to leave, and when I needed you most . . ." she trailed off, more tears of relief and exhaustion spilling down her cheeks.

"I never stopped lovin' ya, Abigail," he said. It wasn't what she expected to hear, but it was still perfect. "I'm sorry I didn't say it outright from the beginning, but that's what kept me comin' back."

"That's very good, because I do too."

"I hate to interrupt," said Adam, "but there's safety in numbers, and I think we should all head back together."

"Agreed," said Ian. "But not too quickly. The room hasn't steadied yet."

Once Ian felt ready to walk, they made their way back to the party to find Mr. Rosenlund. After recounting the events to him, his natural response was, "This is nonsense. Why should I believe what any of you say?"

"You can believe me, sir," said Abigail. "I know what I saw. Just give Adam a minute of your time."

"Forgive me, dear. But you are clearly not in the right state of mind."

"Actually, she is," said Phillip, descending the staircase with the constable. Everyone in the room either stood in a silent state of shock or whispered and pointed as Phillip at last emerged into the open public. "This whole night was a setup, Mr. Rosenlund."

"Phillip," he gasped. "How—?"

Ian, Adam, and Phillip all answered in unison, "It's a long story."

"Would you so kindly direct us to Mr. Deveraux?" asked the constable. "I'm sure you two have spoken during the last hour. With the confession of Bromley Turner, who is now in custody, as well as the reliable evidence obtained, I have cause to put Mr. Deveraux under arrest."

Christopher frowned, letting out a long breath before saying, "I believe I last saw him in the cigar room."

"Thank you," said Phillip, joining the constable out of the ballroom. If they didn't have an audience before, they certainly did after the two returned with Richard in tow, wearing a set of shackles.

Abigail was close enough to see him lean close to Adam and say, "I regret nothing. And this isn't over."

But Adam appeared unaffected as he responded, "Over or not, in the name of Caleb and Lynnette Garrow, *you're* finished."

The constable tugged on Richard's arm, pulling Richard through the parting crowd of whispering gawkers.

Phillip nodded. "Well said."

"Wait, where's Solana?"

"I'm here," said Solana, pushing her way through the crowd of murmuring spectators. "And Phillip, I'm sorry to do this so suddenly. But someone here would really like to see you."

She stepped aside, and Iris emerged. And without any thought of maintaining decorum, she and Phillip rushed to each other, embracing as if the other were life itself.

"I never gave up hope," said Iris.

"The very thought of you kept me alive," he told her.

She smiled through her tears. "You kissed an enchanted princess, remember? Isn't that what makes a man invincible?"

He softly chuckled. "I won't ever leave you again."

Abigail touched a hand to her heart. It was the happy ending Abigail had consistently prayed for on Iris's behalf. At last she could finally rest easy, knowing he was safe.

When Phillip took notice of everyone's gaze directly toward them, he stepped back and cleared his throat. "I'm sure you have a lot of questions."

"All of which can be answered in the privacy of my home," said Christopher. "I'm sure Mr. Chamberlin has had enough excitement at his own party for one night."

"We all have," said Adam. "Solana, have you seen Camden around?"

"I haven't. He disappeared after you and I had our dance."

Adam and Phillip exchanged tired glances. Ian sighed. "Looks like the night isn't over yet, boys."

Adam and the rest of the men searched the grounds for half an hour until they checked the carriages to find Richard Deveraux's was missing.

"He must have fled after seeing the constable take his father," said Christopher. "Though by now I shouldn't be surprised. I'll go to constable and let him know Richard's son has fled the scene."

"For what it's worth, I'm sorry, sir," said Adam, genuinely meaning it. "I know you put all your faith in what the Deverauxs were offering. And I'm sorry you and I never had the chance to start off on the right foot."

Phillip stepped forward, resting a hand on Adam's shoulder. "But with tonight being the night for second chances, I'm here as a witness: Adam was with me when the fire started. He helped me save your daughter."

Adam removed his glove, showing the scars on his hand.

"And by the grace of God," continued Phillip, "he knew where to find me when I was lost."

Christopher sighed, not in frustration or disappointment, but to simply fathom it all. "You mean to say the fire was just a coincidence?"

"It could have been Richard, for all we know," said Adam. "He has a complicated history, with a rumor that his son isn't legitimate. He also had the means to manipulate Bromley into doing his dirty work."

Christopher folded his arms, and Adam watched him take a moment to let this information absorb. But his next question took Adam off guard.

"What intentions do you have with my daughter, Adam?"

Shamelessly, Adam responded, "With all due respect, I very much want to court her like a proper gentleman should."

"With the intention of marriage, no doubt."

"I believe that's up to her. But my adopted father has left me the Burnheart estate and a generous amount of land to raise my own family on. Any woman I choose to be my wife will live comfortably for the rest of her days, as will our children."

"On what support?"

"Mine, as my business partner," said Phillip. "Fairbrooke will be up and running once I re-sign the paperwork."

There was a long and uncomfortable silence after that. Adam frantically searched for anything more to stay, but at last, the truth was out. There was nothing more to share, no more encouraging words to help him in this situation.

"When you have it all in writing, I'd like to see for myself," said Christopher, buttoning his coat. "When I do, you may see Solana. Now excuse me; I would like to update my wife."

He walked off just as Adam opened his mouth to say thank you.

"Would you look at that," said Phillip.

"Did I just receive his permission to court Solana?"

"Not completely, but I do think you have your foot in the door. You are missing one thing, though. You haven't asked *Solana's* permission to court her yet."

Adam smiled. "Not officially. But like you said, I do think I have my foot in the door."

Phillip shook his head and gave Adam a brotherly slap on the back. "Let's go home."

"How do you think Cedric Westmont will take all of this? Do you think he'll allow Abigail to marry Ian?"

"I wouldn't be surprised if he did. Ian will have a pretty substantial income in the coming months as a breeder at Fairbrooke."

Adam smiled. "You don't say."

"I say . . . anything could happen."

Camden Deveraux had never lacked for anything in his life. From the time he was a young boy and through adulthood, Camden was willing to do whatever it took to consistently have the upper hand. It was how the world worked if anyone wanted to thrive, and it was a philosophy his father raised him to live by. And Camden grew to love the feeling of superiority, craved the way it made him feel knowing he could make people smile or cower in his presence with one look. For that, Camden had always trusted his father completely, and he owed him his life for his brilliance and fearlessness.

But the moment he overheard a guest whisper about a constable arriving to arrest Richard Deveraux, Camden felt a wave of panic. When he left to address the constable himself and say some excuse on his behalf, that panic turned to dread upon seeing the Garrow brothers. And, of all people, Ian O'Connor was with them.

This wasn't supposed to happen. His father had everything worked out perfectly, and Camden had been too careful seeing it through. He'd been so close to getting everything he wanted, to destroying their only competition and claiming his prize. But obviously it wasn't enough. His father had been more foolish than he'd expected, and sure enough, Camden would pay the price for it—unless he fled or lied about his involvement.

Impulsively, Camden rushed out of the party, before he could be seen, and found their carriage. "Take me back to Fairbrooke," he ordered.

"What of Mr. Deveraux?"

"Never mind him. Take me home now, or I'll see that you never have a job again."

"Yes, sir," the carriage driver said, opening the door for him.

Alone with his thoughts, he wondered what his father could say to get himself out of this mess. Would he lie? Or would he confess and sell out his own son? Camden had been the one to find Bromley in the first place. It was his idea to help him attack the Irishman in exchange for selling Phillip to the smugglers. The same Irishman who now stood proudly with those two mongrels who just wouldn't die! He should've shot them with his own pistol in the first place. It would have saved Camden from all this complication.

When the coach finally reached Fairbrooke, he stormed inside the grand house, feeling possessive of all that surrounded him. He fumed as he ran to the strongbox, unlocking it to first pack all the money and forms of blackmail his father saved in case something like this happened. He threw the rest of his valuables into a bag and then rushed to the stable for a horse.

Mounting the saddle, he kicked hard on the beast's hindquarters and took off into the night. But just as he exited the gates, Camden kicked harder, and the horse faltered. Suddenly he was in the air as the horse bucked and then reared with a loud whinny.

The world spun until Camden hit the ground, pain exploding in his head.

He grunted and moaned, rolling onto his back, feeling as though karma was finally catching up to him. Camden could easily deny what he had done in front of a judge. But the first act he carried out—the sin he'd carry for the rest of his life—would be his downfall if his father chose to use it against him.

In his injured stupor, Camden gazed into the night sky, recalling the day he'd snuck onto the Garrow's property with a flint and striker. The taste of the liquid courage he drank was bitter, and he poured the rest of it on the trees, following his father's order.

"It's time for Caleb's legacy to fall to ashes," his father had said, and Camden wholeheartedly agreed.

But he hadn't anticipated hearing the cries of a silly girl behind him. "Stop!" she'd shouted. "What do you think you're doing? Put that out!"

Her image had been too hazy to comprehend. He couldn't have any witnesses, so he'd done what made the most sense in his inhibited state of mind. He'd picked up a large stick and swung as hard as he could.

It was the only other time he felt the same dread as he did now. But in her case, she'd turned out fine. News spread of her amnesia, and she never showed any signs of recognition whenever Camden called. This naturally relieved him, but it was his father who found the whole thing amusing and wanted to add to the irony by encouraging Camden to court her. She wasn't at all his type, but he favored the idea of claiming her land. And once they were wed, if she *did* remember what he did, he'd have enough authority over Solana to keep her mouth shut.

Camden thought he'd only been lying in the road a few short minutes, but apparently it had been much longer than that when the sound of pounding hoofbeats grew louder as the horses drew closer.

"Camden Deveraux?" shouted an authoritative voice.

He sat up, twisting himself around to see a uniformed man dismount. The blood rushed from Camden's head, and his head throbbed mercilessly. When his vision cleared enough for him to recognize the constable, he attempted to run. The act was desperate but was not enough to escape. The constable seized his wrists and had him easily bound in shackles.

Right then Camden was resolved to expect the worst, and once more in desperation, he shouted, "It was all my father's doing! I'm the victim in all this!"

"Of course you are," he said sardonically. "Feel free to say so in front of the judge. But I have a feeling you will get exactly what you deserve."

$\mathcal{T}$WENTY-SEVEN

———— ❧ ————

$\mathcal{S}$olana walked the orchard like she did every day this past week since the night of Chamberlin's ball. This time Faye was with her, twirling a yellow leaf between her fingers.

"I cannot wait for Iris's wedding," Faye gushed. "She will look so lovely in her dress, and the party will be dazzling."

"You are quite right," Solana said, chuckling. "But it'll be some time before it all comes together."

"Then it can be a Christmas wedding! Oh, how romantic."

"You know, Faye, it *is* romantic. Snowfall, sleigh bells, warmed apple cider, fireplaces . . . a perfect time for a young couple to be in love."

"Finally we agree on something," said Faye.

Solana laughed, pulling her sister close to her side as they walked. When they reached the courtyard, she didn't miss the horse that hadn't been there earlier grazing in the pasture. When they neared the stable, they both found Adam Garrow feeding an apple to Solana's horse.

When they approached him, he turned and smiled. "Always a pleasure to see the lady of the house," he said with a low bow.

"The pleasure is mine," said Solana.

"Oh, excuse me, I was talking to Miss Faye."

Faye giggled, and Solana inwardly applauded his quick-witted response.

"I like him," Faye said to Solana. "Definitely more handsome than Camden."

"Faye!" she scolded.

But Adam put a hand to his chest. "That is the greatest compliment I will ever receive."

Stifling her laugh, Solana gestured Faye toward the house. "Will you give us a moment?"

Faye shrugged, waving goodbye to Adam before hurrying inside. Solana walked toward the pasture and rested her arms on the wooden gate. "It's nice seeing you here under better circumstances," she said.

"It's nice *being* here under better circumstances. The last week has been productive but full of tension, with Phillip getting back on his feet. Camden was found attempting to leave town. Both he and Richard will be facing trial."

"Is it wrong that I have no sympathy for Camden?"

"I have very little. But only because he wasn't raised to know any better."

"True. I'm glad this whole catastrophe they caused has finally come to a conclusion."

"As am I. There is something you should know, information revealed during Camden's confession. It was he who started the fire. And he is the one responsible for your head injury."

Solana recoiled. "What? How?"

"From what he said, you found him striking flint and tried to stop him. He hit your head hard enough to knock you unconscious and affect your memory."

She wrapped her arms around herself, feeling chills run down her spine. "This is the same man who asked me to marry him?"

"His way of controlling you, it would seem. You didn't remember, but in case you did, Camden would always have his eye on you."

She let out an anguished sigh. Though her memory was too damaged to recall that particular detail, it was the missing piece Solana had been waiting for, and at last the truth had completely fallen into place.

"I knew something wasn't right about him," she said. "And I'm glad I don't remember that particular detail. It would likely haunt me for the rest of my life."

"For your sake, I'm glad as well."

"You must also be relieved. No one can ever doubt that you didn't start that fire."

"I am only relieved that everyone I love and care for is safe. And now I can move forward with my life in peace."

Solana smiled at his words but decided on a change of subject. "My father told me about Burnheart. How's the rebuilding coming along?"

"Wonderful. The final renovations are nearly complete. It lacks furniture, warmth, and utilities. But it has potential."

"Potential is good. You took something that was falling apart and found a way to put it back together. Burnheart will thrive because of it, just like you will thrive."

Adam nodded. "I think I can now. I do think I will plant a few apple trees though. The blossoms would look lovely come spring in a few years. Seeing them will be a perfect reminder of that."

Solana felt heat rise to her cheeks as he said the word "blossom." It was a silly joke between them, but what he insinuated made her feel important to him somehow.

"Adam, why do you wear those gloves so often? I never see you without them."

He shrugged. "They hide my scars."

"You don't have to hide your scars with me."

When their eyes met, Adam removed the leather from his hands and laid them over the fence. His marked skin wasn't ugly to her, but a reminder of what he had sacrificed.

Gently, she placed her hand over his reddened one, and he reached out with the other to brush the hair off the side of her face.

"I once asked you if I could court you formally, if I at all had a fighting chance."

"You did."

"Dare I ask now . . . do I have a fighting chance?"

Solana could have given him a verbal answer, but instead she lifted herself up onto her tiptoes and gently placed her lips against his. They lingered for a moment, as Solana remembered the first kiss they shared. As their kiss deepened, warmth spread throughout her body, and she could revel in the hope of a lasting future with him.

When she pulled back slightly, he muttered, "Is that a yes or a no?"

Solana shook with laughter, feeling him do the same as he wrapped his arms around her. "That is definitely a yes," she said.

"Then right here, I'm making you another promise," he said, resting his forehead on hers. "I promise to make you laugh every day and see to it that you are always happy."

"I'd like that very much. And in return, I'll *occasionally* let you call me Blossom. And if all goes well, I promise that one day I'll help you plant the apple trees. And we can start a new orchard together."

"I can't decide which I like more," he chuckled.

As they walked hand in hand along the countryside, Solana looked at Adam and realized something amazing: fate had a chaotic way of bringing them together, but they had come full circle, rekindling their relationship in a sea of apple trees.

ACKNOWLEDGMENTS

I finished writing *The Burnheart Redemption* at the starry-eyed age of nineteen. Now I'm thrilled to say that after six years, my teenage dream has finally come true! A special thanks to the Cedar Fort crew who had the experience and patience to make that happen. To my fellow authors who gave me wonderful advice. To my quirky and lovable friends and family who inspired this coming-of-age story. And to the handsome male models, who I can claim as dear friends of mine, for being the faces of my three heroes. Each and every one of you rocks.

Cheers to you, XO

$\mathscr{D}$ISCUSSION $\mathscr{Q}$UESTIONS

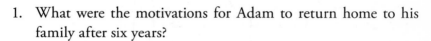

1. What were the motivations for Adam to return home to his family after six years?

2. Why did Adam and Solana want to keep their identities a secret when they first met each other?

3. Why was Solana's family so keen on keeping Adam's existence a secret?

4. The Garrow brothers are certain of a mysterious enemy plotting to overthrow their family's estate. Who are the likely suspects?

5. Who could likely be the lurker in the last chapter?

ABOUT THE AUTHOR

$\mathcal{C}$helsea Curran lives in the desert valley of Arizona. Though secretly a romantic, she used to spend most of her time brooding over the idea of love until her college roommates (now best friends) introduced her to the exciting and fantastic world of romance novels. When she's not teaching, dancing, painting, laughing, or baking cookies, she's in her blanket fort giggling over the handsome hero capturing the fair lady's heart. And no matter how old she gets, that will never change.

Countless authors have inspired to her to write stories for those who seek the same ideas that brought her comfort, joy, and hope for the future. By experience, she believes one good book can change a person's life forever.

Scan to visit

www.chelseacurranauthor.com